Grandmama and The Church of the People

Grandmama and The Church of the People

✦

Keepin' It Real!

A Novel

Minister Yevonne B. Cohen
and
Elder Benton K. Cohen

iUniverse, Inc.
New York Lincoln Shanghai

Grandmama and The Church of the People
Keepin' It Real!

iUniverse books may be ordered through booksellers or by contacting:

iUniverse
2021 Pine Lake Road, Suite 100
Lincoln, NE 68512
www.iuniverse.com
1-800-Authors (1-800-288-4677)

Because of the dynamic nature of the Internet, any Web addresses
or links contained in this book may have changed
since publication and may no longer be valid.

This is a work of fiction. All of the characters, names, incidents, places,
organizations, and dialogue in this novel are either the products of the
author's imagination or are used fictitiously.

ISBN: 978-0-595-45450-1 (pbk)
ISBN: 978-0-595-89762-9 (ebk)

Printed in the United States of America

Inspired by **Psalm 78 v. 1-4,** this engaging series of Lesson-laden vignettes, set in a fictitious, small-town, Negro church in South Carolina over the course of 20 years between 1945 and 1965, serves as a pretext for Grandmama to teach her passel of unnamed grandchildren about the curious ways of the "Good Lord God" … Father, Son and Holy Spirit. Through the telling of her stories, Grandmama unfurls fables about the forms and fashions as well as the fun foibles of faith fellowship at *The Church of the People*, and shows us all that in our human-ness, we will surely fall short of God's perfect ways sometimes, even Grandmama, her own self.

The stories are related in the conversational Ebonics of that era. Grandmama is a woman with a formal education that only reached sixth grade, yet she has a Master's degree in Christian life learning, as taught by the Holy Spirit.

Most of the stories are light and some are "fall out" funny, but others tackle subjects that challenge Christian communities to eschew the worship of denominations, individual churches or charismatic leaders in favor of a real personal relationship with God, the Holy Father of all Creation … God, the Son, who sacrificed everything for the undeserving … and God, the Person of Holy Spirit, who walks and talks with us through the signposts of life, and who can get His feelings hurt when we disobey, in the name of God.

Min. Yevonne B. Johnson, is also author of *"A Miracle in the House"*, a heart-wrenching memoir of a childhood marked by abuse and dysfunction and her eventual healing, through a relationship with God and the embracing of forgiveness. She began this, her second book, before she married Ben Cohen, a born-again Jew and Pentecostal elder. After reading some of her stories, he began to add stories in his own style, which, while different in the literary sense, are in simpatico, so far as his grasp of the character and her faith focus. The stylistic similarities and differences provide texture and contrast without losing the point ... God is ... all the time ... and all the time ... God is ... and that's good news!

INTRODUCTION

WHO IS GRANDMAMA?

Grandmama's real name is Mrs. Gladys Marie Singletary, but everybody in town knows her just as Grandmama, and her secret nickname is Sis. Illgitchagood. Grandmama has been a widow for forty years. She is the mother of three children, two boys and a girl, and Grandmama to a passel of "baby grands", some by blood and some by circumstance. She has a mild temper until someone dares to mess with one of those baby grands … at which point, you've got a tiger by the tail.

Grandmama is a short and pleasingly plump woman with a beautiful round face and dark chocolate skin. Bright-colored scarves, which she wears mostly during the summer months, accent her long, gray tight-curled hair. She sees and hears amazingly well. In fact, the only physical complaint that she makes is that her hips tend to cause her pain, especially if she walks too far in one day. She feels it most during the fall and winter months.

Grandmama lives alone in the small town of Hamletville, South Carolina, if you consider shepherding a passel of grandchildren to and from church on a regular basis, living alone. She has a small gray and white wooden one-story house that is in serious need of a paint job. The porch that she sits on also needs repair, and each time her brown rocking chair, her favorite, moves frontward and backward, you hear alternating creaking sounds from the chair and the porch. Grandmama likes it that way 'cause it keeps nosy neighbors and intruders from sneaking up on her. Still, Grandmama likes to sit there, especially when she shares stories about her church, The Church of the People.

Grandmama Singletary has a full-throttle sense of humor, which is evident as she spins her church stories to family and friends. She can also be somewhat melodramatic, and she has cute mannerisms, which at times make her appear to be half her age, a characteristic townfolk and kin seem to like most about her. It's really fun to hear her tell her stories with such animated and nostalgic enthusiasm, recalling episodes from way back. After all, Grandmama became a Christian at The Church of the People, where she has been a member ever since she was a child when she first received the anointing in the Holy Spirit.

Anyone who is blessed to sit with and listen to Grandmama can see how much fun she is, but there's a private side of Grandmama that shows up at times in her conversations, too. It's a reluctance to talk about certain parts of her life, such as her late husband Pete. Pete Singletary died just after their youngest child was born. Grandmama doesn't talk much about him, except to say that there wasn't a nicer man in the whole wide world than Granddaddy Pete. He was known as a religious man who loved to take care of Grandmama.

The one story that she will tell about the late Pete Single-tary goes way back in time, and each time she tells it, her face really lights up.

"One day," she begins, "a man from down the road from where we lived made a remark about my legs. I don't know if'n he was givin' me a compliment or not. All I do know is he wanted to get my attention. Well, Pete picked up a half a tree branch and hit the man in the head. Regardless, I gotta say … I did then … and still do have nice legs."

That was the last time anybody ever said anything about Grandmama that might be considered questionable. It seems that Pete Singletary—nice as he was and all—left quite a legacy for the rest of us about how a man should protect his wife against insults from anyone.

Next to telling her stories on her porch, Grandmama also loves to sit outside and prepare her favorite vegetables … for canning or for supper on Sunday, which is usually served immediately after church services. Her face glows as she snaps green beans, shells yellow and purple peas, and shucks fresh white and yellow corn that comes right out of the little garden behind her house. When her grandchildren visit, they know they will eat well, 'cause Grandmama is an excellent cook. In fact, everybody in town knows that nobody ... as far as east is to west or north is to south ... can make fried chicken, candied yams, chocolate cakes, collard greens with smoked pork ... and the world's best spoon corn bread ... like Grandmama can. But don't expect her to prepare uppity meals like most Northerners enjoy—tea sandwiches, ice tea with a sprig of mint, sponge cakes, and multi-flavored parfaits. Absolutely not ... 'cause when she cooks, she puts both of her feet and one hand into every dish she prepares. That's why her baby grands and lots of other people in town look forward to visiting Grandmama during the summer months and holidays.

Another thing that Grandmama loves to do is read her Bible, and she doesn't care who comes to her house and sees her reading it. In fact, she's got as many as seventeen Bibles (and several different translations) scattered throughout her 4-room house. Grandmama is quick to warn anyone that she comes into contact with, that the Christian journey is not without steep, sharp hills and dense, rugged valleys. She is a testimony to everyone who knows her ... that the life of a Christian can one day be filled with incredible joy and the next day with great sorrow. However, all in all, one can learn from her, that a Christian must endure regardless of what happens and that the Good Lord God will never leave us or forsake us.

Happy Reading,
Yvonne and Ben

THE WRITING ON
THE FLOOR

So Jesus said to him, "Unless you see signs and wonders you will not believe."

John 4:48

Every year, our Bishop, Bishop Backus would send a guest preacher from a sister church to do the preachin' on a Sunday, and then the next Sunday, we be right back to Rev. Norman, our regular preacher. I love Rev. Norman, but it's exciting to have a guest preacher, 'cause ya just never know—the spirit might be so high, 'bout anything could happen. Heck, Brother Boozer might just get hisself saved.

Children, Brother Boozer is a good instance of a man, a decent man, who just drownded hisself in his bottle of wine and done drownded his kinfolk with him. You ever wonder why he be always sitting in that little balcony area up above the rest of the church folk? Well see, he sweats out his alcohol so bad that ain't nobody wants to sit by him in church.

Now, the Rev. don't wanna treat him just any kinda way, so Bro. Boozer sits upstairs with Jude, that simple child and his momma, and little baby Vivian and her Grandmama. Lord knows, that baby sure got ants in her pants. If she was my child, runnin' and jumpin' around all the time like she be plugged into the power socket, her little pants'd be so hot and tore up, all the ants would be loosed and on the road to freedom. Anyways, you just never know with a guest preacher, and that's what makes it extra special.

Well children, word around was that Evangelist Strong was comin' 'round to preach again, and the last time he come here—it was a good six, seven years ago, people were fallin' out left and right—and they wasn't drunk on wine—they was slayed and sanctified in the Holy Ghost. Now, I don't mean they was slayed dead, children, I just mean they were—well—GONE! So you can see why I'm so excited. I'm surely gonna have to iron up an extra batch of large silk hankies to throw over the ladies legs. Don't be lookin' at me like that! I know I ain't got no official usher post at church, but I been with the Good Lord Jesus so long now, the folks in church just sorta let me to do what I know need be done. And ya know, with my calluses and bunions so bad, they'll never get me doin' that silly high steppin' usherette march they do on Usher Appreciation Day. But I can tell this, those ladies who fall out, their skirts are get-tin' covered up and covered up fast, fast, fast, so long as

Grandmama's gotta hanky to toss. The Holy Spirit gonna be the *only* Flo' Show—and that's fo' sho'!

Well, come Sunday, I was up and ready extra early for church so's I could help with the prayers they do before service to seal up and sanctify the room. If'n you don't, ole Satan mightcould be waitin' to spoil the service. We gotta shoo 'im out right and proper from the get, and ya know, Evangelist Strong won't preach in any church if there be any hint of chit chat or ill-reverence in the sanctuary. So he sent his own team of prayer warriors ahead of him, to pray over the church building and especially over the room he was gonna preach in. I mighta got a little peevish about it 'cept we got that little area just outside the preaching room where we can chitty chat—just so long as it ain't loud. Lord, those prayin' folks were praying hard and powerful and for a good long time before they let any of us in. And we stayed quiet outta respect. Even little baby Vivian seemed to sit put long enough for the deacon to open service in prayer. Now, our Deacon's a good prayin' man and all, but those folks that came with Rev. Strong—they drew power! Poor devil didn't have half a chance in there that Sunday.

Now, everything about that service was high. The spirit in the singin' was high! The praise was high AND the worship was high! Then, Rev. Strong stepped up toward the pulpit from his big blue armchair with the satin and ruffles, and he bent over, closed his eyes and spread his arms out wide—and his whole body started to heave and sway. It was somethin' all right! Anytime we got a guest with a title, like Rev. Evangelist Dr. Strong, he gonna sit in the big chair that usually be reserved for Rev. Norman. But, this Sunday we had Rev. Strong and Rev. Norman was surely gonna miss somethin' else. Then again, he was preaching at some other Reverend's church and the people there was probably excited too, cause they didn't rightly know what to expect—just like us. It's like musical chairs, children, 'cept'n it's musical churches for the preachers.

Anyway, I was really ready for some power-filled preachin'. I even wore some clothes that wasn't quite as nice as the ones I usually wear to church, 'cause I didn't wanna take a chance on fallin' out in my best dress—but you can be sure I was still dressed fine and respectful—just not *too* fine. Some folks in the church might wonder if I'm *really* saved, just 'cause I don't be fallin' out every time a Pastor prays over me. Well, I gotta feel it for real. I'm like Joe Louis. I gotta get hit before I goes down. And, if the spirit ain't movin' me my own self, I ain't takin a dive jesta make *The Man of God* feel like he got power. I don't care what title he be carryin' in the door. The Spirit-move is between me and God alone. Not like sister Millie. She drops so fast folks started callin' her Mildred Falls. Mildred Falls is the name of the lady been playin' piano for Mahalia Jackson all these years. Child, the real Mildred sure could pound those keys—and stomp the devil down doin' it. Anyway, that's the name folks started callin' Sis. Millie, after she jumped the gun fallin' out so regular.

Well, Preacher finally straightened up real slow and gradually lowered his raised arm and stepped up to the pulpit lookin' like a man of purpose. I don't believe he looked that way on purpose—like Sis. Millie be fallin' out on purpose—he just had a mighty serious feel about him. Now, his preachin' voice was deep—not gruff, mind you—but it sorta rattled your ribs when it rose up and beads of sweat be spreadin' 'cross his brow—not all soakin' wet … so's you wouldn't wanna hug him after church or nothin' … but he was surely workin' it. He started his sermon about surrendering to the Spirit". He titled it, "How Far Will You Go, For Grace On Earth and Glory in Heaven". Now, he didn't need to preach it for too long, but he sho' 'nuff preached it STRONG—for his namesake—well, for both him and Jesus' namesakes.

The people was praising and worshipping up a storm when Rev. Strong started fixin' to do his call up for prayer. He took off the black robe he was wearin' and waved to his Armor-Bearer—that's kinda like the preacher's bodyguard and butler—takin' care of him so's he can just hone in on bein' holy and not be bothered with little stuff. The Armor-Bearer came forward carryin' the *full* armor of God, in the way of a sparklin', full-length purple robe with gold silk trim around the neck and around the hem. And I wanna tell ya, that Armor-Bearer looked mighty sharp hisself, in his blue pinstripe suit, white starched shirt with cuff links and plain-tip black shoes shined so bright you could fix your hair in 'em like they was little mirrors. People all over the church were on their knees praying and parsin' in tongue. I was on my toes, hankies at the ready! Then Rev. Strong, he put out the call to come up to the altar. He called people to come up and accept Jesus in their sorry lives and he called people to come up just so's he could pray over their needs—and maybe some mightcould get both—kinda like in that new Chinaman's diner that opened in town, where you get to order something from column A *and* something from column B.

Children, have you ever heard the ladies talk about that Holy Spirit and how it'd be like a burnin' fire shut up inside your bones? Well, don't be afraid. You don't need no fire-man or nothin'. Matter of fact, whenever that spirit puts a move on this old gal, it feels more like a spring of fresh cool water bubblin' up from way down deep inside me. I *mean* to tell you, it be a truly *free* feeling. I don't want to cast doubt on other folk's Spirit feel. Maybe theirs be hot inside, while mines be cool. Either way, the power in that Holy Ghost Spirit is nothing to be trifflin' with. I mean, if people be up there fakin' that stuff they mightcould be fakin' the whole thing and not really be saved at all. Then, that same Holy Ghost Spirit they be tryin' to conjure up, mightcould drop 'em out cold dead on the spot. If the *real* Holy Spirit comes out in ya, the Good Lord God knows it and He don't abide such trifflin'. Now, a lot of white churches have some real Spirit going on. Well, except maybe for those Methodist white folks. I mean, they don't invite the spirit in really—do they now? Matter of fact, some of the white churches don't invite much of nothing inside—'lest it be white like them. I never once felt welcome in they church. Oh, I don't mean no harm, children. White folks got their ways—and their ways might not be *our* ways, anyways. Well, I guess what I'm tryin' to say is that they are still children of God—I s'pose?

Anyway, Rev. Strong started prayin' and prophesyin' in the Spirit over folks, but nobody was fallin' out—well, 'cept Sis. Milllie of course, who dropped like a sack of spuds the minute Rev. Strong started into prayin'—and I'm not so sure that counts. The Rev. would lay hands on folks—slap a big palm on their forehead—lean 'em way back and shout in tongues right in their ear. Now, God is surely able, but wasn't nobody else fallin' out, and the Rev. seemed to be runnin' outta steam after so many folks went up to get a piece of his anointing. Then, I saw Rev. Strong point to the back of the church and he sent out a high-sign to his Armor-Bearer to come up front. I sure could use one of those armor-bearers 'round the house to help me with you little hellions when ya get to messin' it all up. Anyways, Rev. whispered something in the man's ear and the Armor-Bearer walked back to the coat rack at the back of the church and pulled a good size bottle out of the pocket of Rev. Strong coat. I knew that coat belonged to the Rev. 'cause it was a beautiful overcoat—best one on the rack and as good a coat as any coat I ever seen on that old rack. Now, I was prayin' that the bottle wasn't wine or liquor. Bro. Boozer musta been lickin' his chops in case it was but I couldn't see him upstairs. Then I realized it musta been the *anointing oil.* That's it! Rev. just forgot to check the oil in his vessel. Now, it was *really* time to get ready with my fresh pressed silk hankies. I guess you could call me a skirt-chaser, eh children?

After that fine-dressed Armor-Bearer done gave Rev. the bottle of holy oil, Rev. stepped down from the pulpit to get to more of the folks. The Armor-Bearer started back up the aisle and I checked my hair in his shiny shoes as he walked past and noticed little droplets of clear liquid on his shoe tip. Well, just as he came across Sis. Millie, she was sprawled outwide right in the middle of the aisle. But we were used to just workin' around her. Now, Millie wasn't no Skinny-Minnie but she wasn't all too big. Anyway, just as he lifted his black spit-shined shoe to step over Millie, he seemed to slip a little and he tripped over her and heaved forward, fallin' right into Elder Oldham, who was in his usual aisle seat. Elder got pushed right into Sis. Broadnax who was down on her knees prayin', and she was a *very* large women. Children, women that big shouldn't be getting on their knees. Heck, it takes Elder Oldham and Elder Sheppard both to lift her up when she's done supplicatin'. Anyway, Elder Oldham fell head first over Sis. Broadnax, flipped head over heel and kicked somebody ... and that somebody musta got pushed into the wall and knocked down the plaque they put up when the founding Rev. died ... over forty years ago.

Things was happenin' so fast and furious, it was like a hurricane swirlin' around me. And children, you wouldn't believe what happened next. More people started trippin' over people and knockin' folks this way and that—they was fallin' like bowling pins. When the chain reaction finally hit Rev. Strong, he lost his grip on the bottle of anointing oil and it went flying. The front row got a bath in it. There was oil everywhere and the few folks standin' started in to slippin' and slidin'. They was front-slidin' and back-slidin' too—I don't mean fallin' out with the Good Lord God or anything—just fallin' out everywhere in the church. After it was finally all over, every soul sittin' downstairs at the church was sprawled out 'cept'n me. And I didn't wanna start tossin' hankies 'cause there wasn't enough to go around and I didn't wanna mess up my almost-Sunday-best dress. Then there came this loud *WHOOP!* from up in the balcony and everyone's eyes looked up in amazement—even though they was still all sprawled out and oiled up. Children, if I hadn't seed it with my own two eyes, I'da never believed it. Now I know my eyesight ain't what it once was, but I know fo' sho' what I saw—what we all saw—and it was somethin' else!

It was Bro. Boozer jusy a' *WHOOPIN"*. Then, he started into preachin' the sacred Word of the Good Lord God … clean and clear and sober-sounding as a judge … but I mean he was talkin' that *D.D.* talk like he been preachin' all his life. He seemed to know the Word backward and forward and he'd let out a whoopin' wail after each line—like signposts out on the state road. Then, little Simple Jude, who had never uttered a mumblin' word to me nor nobody else far's I know—he was doin' a Holiness dance and praisin' God right out loud. And all the while, little baby Vivian was sitting perfectly still and quiet, with a look of contentment on her chubby little cheeks that even made *me* kinda green … with envy, that is. Then Bro. Boozer pointed straight at me and signaled me to come upstairs, just like I was *his* Armor-Bearer.

Now, I never liked dealing with those narrow, steep little stairs … noway, nohow … but he kept signaling at me … and so I carefully wound my way over and around all the folks sprawled out and dumb-founded on the floor, and I heard Bro. Boozer say, "Everyone be perfectly still for the move of God!" He said it with such authority, that they all just did what they was asked—all except me. I was still navigatin' them rickety stairs. My legs was a might tired and I was a little out of breath, but I was the last saint standing from the downstairs folks and I was glad to get away from that oil spill. I surely wasn't inclined to take a dive.

Well, when I was finally standing right in front of Bro. Boozer, he looked at me straight in my eyes. Matter of fact, he seemed to be lookin' straight through me. He said, "Mother, please close your eyes", and I did. I remember thinkin … I hope everybody had their eyes closed too, so's nobody be lookin' up the ladies dresses that didn't get in on the hanky toss. Anyway, I left all my hankies on my seat downstairs. Then Bro. Boozer rested a gentle hand on my shoulders and slowly turned me around and whispered, "Mother, look down".

When I opened my eyes, I knew I was witness to a true miracle. The people was all sprawled out down below, lookin' just like a huge string of dominoes and children, as Jesus is my witness, the people was strewed out in just such a way, that their bodies layin' together spelled out the letters G—O—D! A miracle to be sure—*THE WRITING ON THE FLOOR!*

THE LORD'S SUPPER

While they were eating, Jesus took bread, gave thanks and broke it, and gave it to his disciples, saying, "Take and eat; this is my body."

Matthew 26:26

This story is about the Lord's Supper. Grandmama said that the day started out just wonderful, it seemed. We asked her, what she meant by 'the day seemed wonderful'? Well, according to Grandmama this is what happened.

One very hot summer morning Preacher Goodenough, who was a rather fine looking, reddish brown-skinned man standing about 6 feet tall with his hair styled like President Abraham Lincoln, had just finished preaching a dynamic sermon. As a matter of fact, the sermon was so good that the 100 people in attendance seemed to have forgotten that they were scorching hot. I tell you it had to be at least 130 degrees in there along with a lot of humidity.

I was sitting on the next to the last pew wearing my beautiful yellow and purple plaid dress. I sat in the back so that I could see what everybody had on and what kind of worship attitude they'd walk into the church with. For me, sitting in the pew next to the back not only made it easy for me to watch everybody from the moment they walked into the church until Sunday service was over, but it also gave me a chance to wink at the preacher while he was preaching. I knew that he liked it 'cause he would say my name while he was preaching.

Chile, the sermon was good but the temperature was getting hotter as the preacher continued to preach. I realized how hot I was by what was happening to my clothes. I tell y'all, my clothes had become so sweaty that it looked as if I had had an accident on myself. Chile, my drawers got so sweaty that it looked like I had lost my bladder.

I don't think I was the only one who could see how hot I was 'cause I happened to look over at old nosy, tall, skinny Sister Dontmissnothin, and I could see that she was really looking at me real hard. When I looked at her she snubbed me, and she had a strange expression on her face. As a matter of fact, she kept watching me, and then she had the nerve to lean over, and it looked like she was telling old midget looking Brother Can'tkeepnothin that I had wet on myself. I knew she said something to him about me 'cause he started leaning over the pew to see for himself. Trust me Chile, I was mad as a firefly on a hot skillet.

When it was time to go up for the Lord's Supper, I was real nervous 'cause I didn't want nobody to think I had wet on myself. So, I asked old short, plump prune faced Sister Fussalot if she would go up there and get my serving of the Lord's Supper for me 'cause I could not get up to do it. I told her that if she got it for me that I could take the Lord's Supper from where I was sitting. But she was in one of her hankty, nasty moods. Chile, she was so nasty that she turned to me with the ugliest look on her face and said that the Lord had jes' told her that he wants everybody to come to the Lord's table for themselves. Boy! Trust me. That made me even madder! So, I turned up my nose and rolled my big, round brown eyes at her.

After that, I had to figure out what to do 'cause I really wanted with all my heart to take the Lord's Supper. So Chile, I decided that I would get up and go to the [outhouse to use the bathroom and then ask somebody to bring the Lords Supper to me out there.] That way, I wouldn't have to go up to the front of the church knowing that people would stare at me. I surely didn't want people to stare or laugh at me. So, I got up to ask one of the men ushers to help me. But as I was approachin' one of the ushers he met me halfway and started in to tellin' me that the Lord had jes' told him something to tell me. He said that the Good Lord God said that I could not take the Lord's Supper to the outhouse. He said that I could not go out with the

Lord's Supper, especially if I was also going to use the toilet. Trust me, by now I was real upset 'cause I truly wanted to take the Lord's Supper, even if I had to do it in the out-house.

Now, I did not want to disobey The Good Lord God or the usher, who was appointed by God, I suppose. Most of all, I didn't want to be struck down by the Good Lord God 'cause, even the Bible says that obedience is better than sac-rifice. So to avoid any major fuss, I wanted to do what God tells all of us to do in the Bible.

With some hesitatin', I got up and went down to get the Lord's Supper, thinking in my mind, "Lord, please don't let me have to turn around and give somebody the back side of my left hand if they laugh at me."

Chile, just as soon as I rose up and started moving toward the front of the church, everybody started laughing at me. I mean they really laughed hard! And it got even louder. Truly, I was shamed 'cause I knew that they thought that I had wet on myself. Meanwhile, as I listened to the cacklin' from everybody, I said to myself I would get them back 'cause, after all, my nickname is Sister Illgitchagood. As I walked away from getting the Lord's Supper, I turned and asked them why they were laughing. Then that thinks she so cute Mrs. Lulafrenchtoast said, "You done wet on your self, didn't you Sister Illgitchagood?" I said, "What are you talking about? I ain't wet myself 'cause you see I fell in the Baptism pool on the side of the church this morning." (There is no pool on the side of the church). "So, Mrs. Lulafrenchtoast, mind your own bidness!" As soon as she looked at the expression on my face and my tone of voice she knew that I was five seconds from giving her the back-side of my left hand. So, she wisely turnt 'round and started talking to somebody else.

In fact, everybody else did the same thing 'cause they caught the hint and decided to leave me alone. Well, after that I guess I showed them! After I got the Lord's Supper, I went and sat down and took the holy meal with everybody else. After all the commotion, I really needed to go out to relieve myself. So I did!

THE OFFERING

"In everything I did, I showed you that by this kind of hard work we must help the weak, remembering the words the Lord Jesus himself said: 'It is more blessed to give than to receive.'"

Acts 20:35

One cool Sunday morning it seemed as though most of the people at church were in good spirits, Grandmama said. We asked her what she meant by good spirits? This is what she told us.

Chile, we had a wonderful service until it came time for the offering. It seemed as though when Preacher Donttakenoguff said the Lord does not like thieves and that nobody should hold nothin' back or the Lord gonna strike 'em dead … like he did Sophinia and Anantube in the Bible. Then what seemed to be a good service at the start of the morning turned cold and suspicious later. That was 'cause some of the people wanted to cheerfully give to God, but some did not. How I knew this was 'cause, when I was on my way to the outhouse at the rear of the church, I saw Brother and Sister Cheaper tiptoeing toward the gray shabby shack that was about two inches away from the outhouse. I knew that they had something devious on their minds 'cause of the way they was movin' … like they was gonna walk up on a snake and surprise it. Anyway, I decided that I would get as close to the shack as possible 'cause I needed to know exactly what they was up to. Well, I did get close enough to put my ear against the wall so that I wouldn't miss a thing that they be sayin'.

Chile, I thought that I would fall over when I heard what they were in there conjuring up. Do you know that those two were in that shack planning to cheat God? I am so glad that I was where I was, 'cause it proves that my gut was right (the Holy Ghost dwells in my gut, ya know). I learned how to hide real well when I was a little girl. Chile, I was the best hide-and-go-seeker in the whole countryside.

Anyway Chile, I could see the two crooks through the hole in the wall close by me. As I peeped into the dark, shadowy shack I saw Sister Cheaper say to her husband Brother Cheaper, "Honey, don't put all the money in the offering tray 'cause you know we have to go out to the club Friday night. And you know the jook joint's gonna cost us at least ten whole dollars for the whole night. So honey, please don't put all the money in the offering tray." I heard her say, "Okay baby, I won't put it all in there." So that is how I knowed that don't everybody put they money in the offering tray for the Good Lord God like they oughta. And I believe that is why the spirit went cold in the church.

So some time later, Preacher Donttakenostuff said the Holy Ghost showed him who was the cause of the service going cold 'cause they didn't wanna give to the Good Lord God. Everybody turned and looked at each other wonderin' who he be signifyin' 'bout. Nobody but me knew what and who was making the service cold. I said to myself, Boy! I hope and pray that Sister Cheaper and her husband don't mess around and end up in hell, as the day is so nice and cool and it would be bad to leave this nice, cool day to go to hell. If they go to hell, they are going to end up with Sophinia and Anantube, who were already in hell. Well, the preacher said, "I'm going give you all a chance to confess and give proper to the Good Lord God." But, Sister Cheaper and her husband had the nerve to pretend like they didn't know nothin' 'bout it. As a matter of fact, the scoundrels sat there with smug looks on their faces. I just couldn't believe what was happening. Don't you know they had a chance to change their plan, but they didn't? No, Chile. They sat cool and straight-faced on the pew across from me, and they didn't say nothin'. Shortly afterward, Brother Cheaper got up and put two little coins in the tray. I knew there were two coins 'cause I heard 'em clink into the offering tray.

But Chile, as soon as he put in those two little coins, as God is my witness, the sky went black, the floor of the church got to movin', the pews started separating from the floor, and the candles that were burning during service went out. Chile, right at that moment, Sister Cheaper and Brother Cheaper dropped dead in front of everybody. I was so scared that I reached into my purse and got out the egg money that I was holding for the market, and then ran as fast as I could up front where the ushers was standing, and put my last five little coins right into the money tray for the Good Lord God.

Trust me Chile, I was not the only one running up there neither. Brother Neveryoumind got to runnin' towards the front of the church to the ushers, too. But he started coughing, and that slowed down his pace. I guess he was nervous. And Chile, when he started coughing his dentures flew right out of his mouth and hit Sister Runhermouth smack in her nose. Chile, everybody got to laughin' at Brother Neveryoumind, but he didn't care 'cause he just kept on runnin' up to the ushers to put his money in the money tray. Boy, I tell you, when Brother and Sister Cheaper dropped dead it caused a whole lot of us to make a beeline for the money tray.

Lord knows I heard them coins clinkin' in the tray for the Good Lord God so fast, it sounded like firecrackers on the 4th of July. I guess those folks really didn't want to go to hell with Sister Cheaper and her husband, who went to join Sophinia and Anantube, you know the two in the Bible that dropped dead and done gone straight to hell.

Well, after that, thank the Good Lord God, everybody was in good spirits once again, 'cause they gave to the Lord's offering, and after all the commotion simmered down, Brother Neveryoumind was able to find his false teeth. Praise the Good Lord God, Chile, the spirit in the Church of the People was even better after that.

THE PASTOR'S ANNIVERSARY

Matthew 23:1-7 Then Jesus said to the crowds and to his disciples: "The teachers of the law and the Pharisees sit in Moses' seat. So you must obey them and do everything they tell you. But do not practice what they preach. They tie up heavy loads and put them on men's shoulders, but they themselves are not willing to lift a finger to move them. "Everything they do is done for men to see: They make their phylacteries wide and the tassels on the their garments long; they love the place of honor at banquets and the most important seats in the synagogues; they love to be greeted in the marketplaces and to have men call them Rabbi.'

Matthew 23:1-7

Well, like just about every other time Grandmama told us about, the pastor's anniversary started out as a wonderful day. You guessed it? Something went wrong ... *again!*

Chile, it was Pastor Shonuffine's anniversary, and everybody seemed to be having a wonderful time until the most craziest thing happened. Chile, everybody was seated and about ready to pray over the meal when one of the members of our church named Sister Can'tget'nufftoeat, who was wearing a red and blue jumper dress and knee high stockings, jumped up and started shouting. Just as she jumped up, the floor started in to shakin' and the tables began movin' all 'round the place. Everybody stopped getting ready to pray and looked at her 'cause she was a big woman. Yes, she was about 400 pounds ... on a good day.

One of the visiting pastors that was sitting down at another table asked what was her problem? Sister Can'tget'nufftoeat overheard what he said and spit back, "What do you mean, what is my problem? I don't have no problem. Looks to me that *y'all* gots the problem."

Then Pastor Shonuffine asked her, "What do you mean Sister Can'tget'nufftoeat?"

"All right," she said. "I am going to tell y'all what is wrong with me. Please tell me, why do all of you preachers get the best food and we get the what's left food?"

"What are you talking about?" Pastor Shonuffine asked her?

"You know darn well what I mean. Look, you and your preacher pals ... y'all got the best sweet potatoes ... the best collard greens ... the best fried chicken ... the best mashed potatoes ... the smoothest gravy ... the sweetest lemonade ... the freshest fried green tomatoes ... the best pound cake ... the whitest table clothes and the prettiest napkins.

"Why is it that y'all got the best food and we got the worst sweet potatoes ... half cooked-looking collards ... dried up fried chicken ... lumpy mashed potatoes ... rocky road gravy ... sour lemonade ... greasy green tomatoes ... a holey table cloth and no napkins ... and we don't have *any* pound cake. And why do you suppose that is?

"Is it causing y'all to think that 'cause you are the pastors and the prissy first ladies and the like, that y'all supposed to get the best food? If it is, well, I don't think so! And I don't know about the rest of y'all standing up over there looking hungry, but just look at the food they think we supposed to eat. It's up to y'all to just keep standing there or decide to sit down and eat that funky food. But I tell all y'all, I'm going to sit down right over there with the pastors and the prissy pastor's wives, and I'm gonna sho'nuff eat ... and eat good!

"Yes, I *am* gonna eat, and I ain't scared that God gonna strike me dead for eating with them, 'cause, the Word of God said He prepared the table for *all* his children ... and that means me too! And you and the rest of y'all pastors and the Prissy pastor's wives can't stop me. Anyway, I don't know who told y'all that you be better than anybody else in this church. Betcha bottom dollar, based on the Word of the Good Lord God, you ain't. Y'all better know that y'all really ain't no better than me."

Chile, don't you know after that squawking, that woman had the nerve to sit down with the pastors and the pastor's wives. I heard her say to everybody sitting at the special table, "Don't keep staring at me, else your food mightcould get cold. Lets eat!"

And then she turned around and looked at everybody else and said, "Don't the rest of y'all cowards just stand 'round wonderin' if I done lost my mind. No, I ain't lost my mind! I'll show y'all that I *am* in my right mind. I am going to eat at the reserved table." After that she said, "Somebody please pass me them there peas and sweet potatoes. Oh! And please don't eat all of the pound cake 'cause I been waiting on it since I laid my eyes on it when I came in the dining room."

THE VISITING
CHURCH CHOIR

Come, let us sing for joy to the Lord; let us shout aloud to the Rock of our salvation. Let us come before him with thanksgiving and extol him with music and song.

Psalm 95: 1-2

Chile, did I tell ya 'bout the time the visitin' choir from up north come barnstormin' through. They was from our nation's capitol in Washington, D.C. and they was gonna stop by our little church and sing ... and our own home church choir was gonna sing too! Sure as I got Jesus in my soul, I wasn't gonna miss it ... not for nothin' in this world. And Lord knows, it was a wild ride!

Chile, it was the church's special day! There was about 25 People in our choir ... men and women ... and every one 'em wore a wig 'cause none of them had any good hair, 'cause 'round' here, it's too hot to keep your hair fixed on your head ... so our choir members wore wigs ... nice wigs too! Just never you mind If'n I be wearin' a wig or no ... ain't nobody's bidness ... most of all some little whippersnappers like y'all.

On this special day, the Church of the People was expectin' this travlin' choir and their pastor for a congregational visit. Sister Know-it-all's sister-in-law, Mother Bell, let on that their Pastor looked like a little fat penguin. She sneaked a peek of the man whiles he and our Pastor, Pastor Rush had dinner. Mother Bell hires herself out to cook for folks when important company wants to eat. They can even put in a request and Sis. Bell can probably ring it up to her recollection. She was dead on it too, Chile, cause when I saw him I thought I would fall out in the middle of the wooden church floor. He looked just like she said ... a little fat penguin. In fact, he looked like his name, which was Pastor Chauncy Chitterling. He was a short, plump, cheerful looking man with a beautiful shiny new pompadour do. Anybody could see he looked like he loved to eat. I'll bet he couldn't let a single little chicken leg fly by his eye. As a matter o'fact, I hear that his favorite dish is boiled and fried chittlins and sweet potato pie with whipped cream on top.

Anyway, the visiting choir arrived, and Chile, let me tell you them folks sure had on some fine robes. They was white with blue and green writin' on 'em and had bright blue trim ... in braids. The robes even had hoods on 'em for some reason. No, wasn't no KKK ... they was each and every one of 'em colored folks.

The man that was runnin' the program, was Brotha Caneitgitnothin'right, a tall, thin dark-skinned man with four of his front teeth missin'. Chile, he had two top teeth missin on the left side of his smile and two bottom teeth missin' on the right side of his smile. Every time I'd be lookin' his way I would have to drop my head so's nobody would catch me laughin' at 'im. Your cousin Calvin coulda drove his John Deere right through that rocky gap. Now, I know that aint Godly, but what can I say? I have to tell the truth don't I? He was the best tither in the Church of the People ... that's why he was runnin' the show.

Let me tell you, when he stood up to bring on the visitin' choir, out of the side of my left eye ... that's my good eye ... I could see his po' homely-lookin wife holdin' her head down a might, 'cause she knew that he couldn't get one dang thang right ... no not one! Chile she looked like she didn't want to be there at all ... at least for right then and right there, anyway. Whilst Brotha Can'tgitnothin'right fumbled his way through the welcome speech, the visiting choir started marchin' up the center aisle towards their seats. Chile, let me tell you again, they sho 'nuff looked fancy and fine. I wish y'all coulda been there, 'cause the way they marched up there ... doin' the holy ghost stroll ... movin from one side then to the other ... right down the aisle. I tell y'all the robes was swingin' like wind. They sat down in their places to wait for their turn to sing 'cause our choir wanted to sing the first song to the visitin' choir, "Welcome to the House of the Lord." Our choir was sittin' in the first two rows on the right side of the church. Now that wasn't where they usually be sittin', but they had to give the visiting choir the place where our choir usually sits up in front. Aint that what right good Christians s'posta do? Chile, and wouln't ya know, just as Brotha Can'tgit-nothin'right stood up to announce our choir, I could see his 'po wife slidin' down in her chair so's like she wanted to bury her sorry self under the pew in front of her. 'Po thang!

Right after that, the visiting choir stood up and the lead singer, a short, stocky coffee-color gal, moved to the center and started to sing one of my favorite Good Lord God songs, "I Know I Got Jesus and That's 'nuff". Chile, my good leg got ta shakin' … my head got ta bobbin' … and I couldn't hardly help myself! … if you know what I mean. 'Bout half way through the first chorus the rest of the choir come in behind her, and they like ta knock the roof off the church of the People.

She just 'bout finished up that song when one of the men in the choir … a great big strappin' man … got up and tore right into his version of "Sign Of The Judgment". That's when our choir started getting happy … real happy! Chile, I mean they near 'bout lost It! It seemed like the pews where our choir was sittin' was on fire. You know like Jeremiah said, "it's like fire shut up in my bones." Let me tell you, I thought I was near 'bout like Enoch … like I was goin' straight on up to heaven. Believe me, I was right in the light of the glory! Chile, our choir joined right in singin', right from where they was sittin! I tell you it was sho 'nuff getting hot up in the House … the House of the Good Lord God, that is! As if that wadn't hot enough, when he was done, the whole choir started in to singin' "Somethin's Got A Hold Of Me". It was like sparks flyin' high on the 4th of July … like we was all plugged into the Power.

The next thing I knew, the Holy Ghost grabbed holt of some of the singers … in both choirs … they got ta jumpin' and shoutin' and flailin' their arms and legs about … hittin' each other … and I mean the wigs and the hair pieces was just slidin off their heads in all shapes and sizes. Boy, the fur was really flyin'. Even Brotha "Peg Leg" Lance, the man who come home from the war with a wooden leg … even he was dancin' up a storm. Chile, I tell you we was havin' a Holy Ghost hullabaloo. Like I said, seems like wigs and hairpieces got to flying this-a-way and that. The wigs got to flyin' off people's heads and the folks in the audience started into laughin'.

Let me tell y'all, outta my bad eye, I could barely see Sister Honeycomb's beehive wig come flyin' into the pastor's wife's face. She had to duck out the way. But she was laughin' and having a good time in the Lord. As best I could see out my good eye, sister Honeycomb's head looked like she had little bitty braids with a thousand red and yellow hairpins stickin' out all over it. I wish y'all coulda been there, 'cause it was a real sight watchin' her make that bee-line for that beehive wig. Chile, the whole church was buzzin!

Then, right in front of me Brotha Bushneck's hairpiece … it looked kinda like Nipsy Russell's hair … a little bit too long for a church brotha … if you know what I mean … it went flyin' and floppin' through the air … like a mini magic carpet … but there was no magic genie steerin' that ship of Zion. Chile, all I could see was him racin' down the aisle … and wouldn ya know … that little rug done fell right into the collection plate. The way he was movin' you could tell … he been runnin for Jesus a long time! From the way he was hound-doggin' that hairpiece, you could see for sho he didn't wanna tithe that piece … even if bush came to shove. By that time, the whole church was hoppin'. And wouldn't you know, Pastor Chitterling's shiny new pompadour looked like a shootin' star comin' offa the Little Dipper … the little gravy dipper, that is. And Pastor was bald as a cue ball in a pool hall. Help me Jesus, I ain't makin' this stuff up.

Then out of my bad eye, I could see Brotha Peg Leg Lance jump straight up in the air and kick his heels. And wouldn't you know, he come down ... on solid ground ... on one lone leg. Chile, that old peg leg of his went flying straight across the pews and out the front door of the church and you could see ... he was hoppin' mad ... and Holy Ghost glad ... all at the same time. I suppose Pastor Chitterling must have thought nuff's enuff. He stood up and started shoutin out somethin' ... over and over again ... but we couldn't hardly hear what it was he be shoutin' 'cause we was so happy ... slayed in the spirit and that choir was soundin' so good!

Then all of sudden, I started feelin' a strong coolin' kinda breeze, and I turned 'round to see where it was comin from and it was comin in through the same door that Brotha Lance's Peg Leg went flyin' out through. Don't you know that the trees started in to rustlin' ... it was like you could hear the wind. One by one, folks started simmerin' down ... and before we all knew it, the only voice we could hear was Pastor Chitterling repeating, over and over again, "IN THE NAME OF JESUS! IN THE NAME OF JESUS! Little by little, you could feel a sorta "Peace Be Still" in his voice, as each wigless person found sweet reunion with they wayward rugs ... in decency and in order. Now, after everybody got theyselves situated in their right place and in their right mind ... our pastor, The Right Reverend R. Randolph Rush stood to do the only thing left that could be done. He gave the benediction saying:

"To everything there is a season, and a time to every purpose under the heaven. (Ecclesiastes 3:1).

And Pastor said,

Children of the Good Lord God—there is a time to get happy ... and a time to be still ... and ... In the Name of Jesus ... we thank The Good Lord God for both.

Then Pastor Rush asked Pastor Chitterling to have the visitin' choir sing, "I'll Fly Away" And, as they began to sing, the wind suddenly changed direction and swept out the door just like it swept in ... and everybody ... humbly ... and with right reverence for the Good Lord God ... left out. Children, I gotta say, the happ'nins was a might hairy for awhile there, but The Good Lord God has His way of bringin' peace in the midst of any storm.

THE VISITING
PREACHER AND HIS
FAMILY

One that rules well his own house having his children in subjection with all gravity. For if a man know not how to rule his own house, how shall he take care of the church of God?

1ˢᵗ Timothy 3:4-5

I remember real well the story that Grandmama told us was about the visiting preacher, his wife and their passel of children. Once again, she said that the day started out just wonderful, it seemed. And as usual, we asked her what she meant by it seemed like everything was wonderful. Well, this is what Grandmama told us.

Chile, the church members had heard a lot about this preacher named Pastor Luther Luvalot, his wife, First Lady Vivian Luvalot ... but from the looks of things, her name need to be Sista Tiredofhavinbabies, cause they got at least eighteen young'uns … least ways that's how many I counted. Coulda have been more for all I know. The young'uns looked like they was 'bout from one and a half to prob'ly least thirteen. Chile, it looked like one was close to two, a little round brown, bowleg butterball baby boy. I knew he was bowleg just from the way she had 'em 'cross her shoulder. Then chile, I saw the *first* set of triplets … you heard me right, the first set, 'cause there was least *three* sets of 'em. There was gals 'bout four years old, long pale and thin as a rail … just like they mamma. Folks say, dark skin pastors like to marry light skinned womens. Then the next troop of triplets was 'bout nine … years old that is … a gigglin' gaggle of gum chewin' gals. You could tell that ain't nobody took to care for those gals hair, 'cause it looked like they musta tied up they own hair in rubber bands. The last set of triplets looked to be 'bout thirteen. They was all boys with nappy, 'knotted-up, not-cut heads of hair. From the minute I seen 'em they was rough-housin' in the house of the Good Lord God. If'n they'da been mines, I would have snatched em' up by they nappy heads and slapped some right respect into 'em … but they weren't mines … thank God!

Chile, believe it or not, that's just the beginnin'. Then they had four sets of twins. Two sets of twins was squozzed betwixt the four year olds set of triplets and the nine year old set of triplets. The first pair was boys 'bout five years old. You couldn't tell 'em apart 'cept for they eyes. Chile, one of em's eyes seemed like the po chile was lookin' left and right at the same time. Lord, that was sho'nuff a sight to see ... Lord Please forgive me. I know that aint right ... or left. Then there was another set of twins ... girls 'bout seven or so. They looked like each other 'cept one thing. One girl spent most of time pickin' her nose with her left hand and the other one was pickin' her nose with her right hand. Chile, you can't dig no deeper in the storehouse than what they was doin'. At the repast after service, if'n those nasty little nose-pickers goes anywhere near the food, I'm gonna hav'ta pass ... on the repast. Lord I know you getting tired of me askin' for forgiveness, but please keep 'em away from the food ... least 'til I get mines.

The other two sets of twins was squeezed twixt the nine year old set of triplets and thirteen year old set of triplets. The first pair was boys ... looked just the same ... 'cept one was so pigeon toed he was trippin' all over hisself ... and the other was so slew foot, he was trippin' up everybody else. Forgive me again Lord, I know fo' sho' I need you to help me walk right ... even if those boys sho'nuff Can't. Then the last pair was girls. They features was just the same the nose ... the ears ... the mouth ... 'cept for one thing. One was coal black and the other one coulda' passed for white folks. Lookin at em made me hungry ... real hungry. It done brought to my mind that double fudge, double layer chocolate cake with the big scoop of vanilla ice cream I churned up to put on it for supper last night. Chile, I coulda ate them gals up … forgive me Lord, but they looked good 'nuff to eat.

Now you can understand why I call her Sista Tiredof-havinbabies. She looked like she aint had no sleep or a minute's peace for I don't know how long time. Chile, she had bags under her eyes that were at least three inches wide and five inches long. She had a humped over back and her hair look like she aint touched it since that first set of trip-lets was born. Po' thang, her dress was full of wrinkles. Her shoes done looked shoddy too. Must be 'cause she been runnin' down that rash of rug rats for the last ten or fifteen years. Po' thang … she just got here and the minute she sat in the pew, she fell dead out to sleep. The two-year-old baby girl she had cross her shoulder musta know'd it was time to take her leave, 'cause she started slowly crawlin' down off her mamma and before you knew it, we heard this little thud 'cause she musta hit the floor … and her mamma didn't move a peg. Chile, that baby got to crawlin' under the pews untyin' folk's shoes, slobberin' her own special spit shine on folks fine Sunday footwear. Chile, that baby was all over the place crawlin' and cooin' havin' a good ole time, while her daddy was preaching. You could see that Preacher Luvalot tried to get his wife's attention, but she was down for the count. She was too tired to get the baby. The other young'uns didn't seem to notice their daddy either, 'cause they was too busy just doin' whatever they darn pleased.

So, Preacher Luvalot just kept on preachin' and keeping his eyes on the Word whilst all the young'uns was doin' what they pleased. Chile, there was so much commotion it looked like a full-out free-for-all. I really couldn't hear what he was preaching 'bout 'cause those young'uns was goin' buck wild in the House of The Good Lord God! Chile, that was too much distraction to pay attention to the sermon.

Then, if that wasn't bad 'nuff, one set of triplets started runnin up to the choir stand and got to pullin' down the songbooks off the racks and pullin' up on the loose floor boards. I tried my best, as God is my witness, to just sit there and try to be still. Chile, I wanted to scream to the Good Lord God for help. Trust me, all I wanted was to hear the Word. The little bit I heard sounded like pretty good Word, but it was too much hubbub in the House. Chile, believe me, I sure wished that I could have figured out what he was preaching 'bout.

I couldn't take much more, so I decided to step outside. At least, I thought I could get some peace and quiet out there, and maybe I could hear some of the sermon from there. But Chile, just as I was on my way out there, I looked up and saw the younger twin boys danglin' from the hangin' ceiling lights. Darned if nobody was trying to get 'em to come down, including Preacher Luvalot his own self. He just kept on preaching. I still don't recall what he was preaching 'bout 'cause those children was all over the place, and the preacher's wife, First Lady Tiredofhavinbabies, had started into snoring ... and believe you me, it sounded like a root hog in heat. Forgive me Lord, I just hear it that a way. I gotsta calls 'em as I sees 'em.... and it tweren't very ladylike neither. Po' thang, she was jesta dog tired ... or hog tired.

I finally made it outside and decided to stay out there 'cause those children were pluckin' my last raw nerve. Chile, like I said, I was hopin' that I would hear the preacher's sermon from outside, but that didn't help neither ... 'cause of those darned children of his. The whole time I was out there, I still never heard what in the world he was preaching 'bout.

Later, after I realized that I wasn't gonna have no peace ... inside or outside the church, I said to myself, "Self, just go and sit on the bench on the side of the buildin'." As I went to sit down, Chile, I looked in the church window and I could see seven of Preacher Luvalot's little hellions runnin' 'round the church screamin' at the top of they lungs ... and chile ... you shoulda seen the ushers chasin' 'round after 'em ... pantin' and prayin' all at the same time. I tell y'all, if I wasn't' no Bible totin' woman, I mightshoulda grabbed holt of a hellion or three and gave 'em the backside of my left hand, but I knew I couldn't' catch 'em as fast as they was movin'. Po' Sis.Tiredofhavinbabies, was still too far gone. She sounded like a rusty sawmill ... like I said, I was too tired to grab 'em and make 'em sit they sorry behinds down somewhere.

It seemed like The Man of God had been preaching near 'bout forever. Chile, I can't tell you the last time that I was in a church and a preacher preached that long. It wasn't bad enough that he preached so long as it was that I still never figured out what in God's creation he was preaching bout. I never could understand a mumblin' word he was preachin.

I read in a magazine once that in the ole days they used to pay book writers by the word ... so, maybe he thought that's how he mightcould get hisself a few extra dollars to feed that herd of hellions of his. Then again, maybe he was holdin' out 'til the hellions wore theyselves down. I gotta admit, deep down inside my heart I was prayin' to the Good Lord God that He would raise a mighty hand ... not to strike 'em down ... but at least to slow 'em up. I was getting' wore out just watchin' em. Chile, can you imagine livin' with that mess day in and day out?

I remember when I was a little gal with all my brothers and sisters ... and when we'd get crazy, mamma would pray," Lord give me strength" and we thought fo' sho' she wanted extra super power to hit us with. I know now that's not what she was prayin' for, but it sure put the fear of God in us just thinkin' about it, and we would quiet right on down, lest we get walloped ... or so we thought. Now I am more like *my* Grandmama was. I aint gotta raise my voice. Alls I gotta do is throw my hands on my hip, cock my head back and to the side and stare 'em down long and strong ... and they knows I mean bidness.

I hate to say it, but I had to leave the service early, 'cause 'nuff's 'nuff. Preacher Luvalot just kept on preaching, and it seemed that we was never gonna get to the benediction and leave out proper. Here I was ... I was walking away from my church ... the Church of The People. I looked back through the open window 'round the side of the church and saw those rowdy rascals ... looked like two sets of triplets and a pair of twins was jumpin' over the pew seats like horses jumpin' the hurdles at the county fair. And don't you believe for a minute the Holy Ghost had' em jumpin' like that. Chile, I thought I would fall out on the ground in my pretty light pink, satin church dress, that I only wore when we had special guests comin. I may as well been wearing an apron and a kerchief. I couldn't believe that those rascals was desecratin' the House of the Good Lord God. Still, with all that mess going on ... the preacher preachin' ... the young'uns runnin' and jumpin' all over the place ... out of control ... First Lady Tiredofhavinbabies sprawled out sawin' wood. I guess she was just plum too tuckered out to do somethin' ... anythin' ... to set that rash of rascals right.

Finally, I got far 'nuff away from the church that I couldn't hear those rascals tearing up the Church of the Good Lord God no more.

After all that commotion, it seemed so silent and peaceful. I hear tell an hour or two after I left, Preacher Luvalot was still up there preachin', and the whole congregation, including all seventeen of those rascals, had fallen out to sleep. Chile, Brother Brooms, the church janitor told me that when he came in to work that Sunday evenin', he thought everybody woulda done left out the church, so's he could clean up. Brother Brooms told me everybody in the church had fallen asleep, 'cept for preacher Luvalot, who was still preachin and Sister Tiredofhavvinbabies who had just woke up from her righteous rest. She never knew that all hell done bust loose while she was snoozing.

It wasn't 'til I got home and was rootin' through the handbag I took to church that mornin', that I found out the title of the sermon I never did hear. You see, right on the program where they announced the visitin' Pastor, it had the title of the longest sermon I never heard …"Don't Forget The Family Prayer" … and he sho' needed all the prayer he could get … if you know what I mean? I found out later, from Sister Can'tkeepnothin'toherself, the church blabbermouth, that she growed up with Sister Tiredofhavinbabies before she married Pastor Luvalot. Sis tells it that Sister Tiredofhavinbabies was only forty years old … and she looked near as old as me. I hear tell she had been a beauty queen when she was twenty-one. Now twenty-one babies later, po' thang, looked wore down to the nub. Chile, I know the Good Book says us right Christians s'posta be fruitful and multiply, but I don't think He meant all of the fruit to come from one single little fruit tree. Po' thang!!

Don't you know, if'n I ever get a chance to see Pastor Luvalot again, I'm gonna set him right down and read what St. Peter said in chapter three verses 4 and 5 about what preacher's families are s'posta be like ... and it aint what I saw that Sunday.

One that ruleth well his own house, having his children in subjection with all gravity. For if a man know not how to rule his own house, how shall he take care of the church of God?

1st Timothy 3:4-5

THE ALMOST FINAL
RESTING PLACE

◆

(Can't No Knave ... Keep My
Spirit Down)

They are the kind who worm their way into homes and gain control over weak willed women, who are loaded down with sins and are swayed by all kinds of evil desires, always learning but never able to acknowledge the truth.

2nd Timothy 3:6

Children I want y'all to know something about life. They say, ain't but two things we can be sure of in this life—death and taxes—and both of 'em can put a serious hurt on ya if'n you don't take care of bidness while you're here in this crazy world. Now mind ya, death aint nothin' to be scared of. Sometimes livin' is scarier than dyin' ...'specially for us Negroes. And the Good Lord God has His own way of takin' the sting outta death ... for us right Christians, that is. It says in the Good Book, if'n we trust our life to Jesus Christ and have faith in Him, and confess that we aint no kinda good without Him, then, when we die, we will be in heaven ... sittin' right near the Good Lord God.

The reason I am tellin y'all children this is 'cause I want to tell ya about a funeral for a heathen rascal and a bounder. He may have told some folks that he was a Christian ... saved sanctified and filled with the Holy Ghost ... but real church folks can tell when someone is sold-out to Satan ... just by the things they say and do ... and the way they treat folks. Everybody be born bad, just like the rest of us sinners, but if'n you don't do nothin' to set your ship right ... it's goin' down and you goin' down with it, Cap'n! It seems this man just went through life doing any old thing ... any old way ... wherever and whenever he wanted ... and it didn't make him no never mind who got mixed up in it nor who got theyselves hurt by it. And children, that ain't no Christian ... no kinda way ... I don't care what nobody say.

The Good Book makes it right clear. We all gonna reap just what we sow ... and that's so ... fo' sho' ... that goes for the rich and the po'. That means a president, or a king or even a man of the cloth. God ain't no kinda respecter of persons. We s'posta be respectin' Him jes' for bein' the

Good Lord God, and we all got to live right or die goin' straight down to hell.

Children, there was this one man we use to see in and around these parts goin' on thirty years and his name was Otis Pride, but everybody called him Buster, Buster Pride. Now we hear tell that he had thirty young'uns or more by at least ten different womens ... and some of 'ems was even married to good church-goin' mens when Buster had his way with 'em.

Hear tell he could sweet talk the po' ladies into doin anything he wanted them to do ... including layin' up in *their* bed, eating *their* food ... and some of 'em even gave this man cash money to go doin' whatever he wanted with it. Dang fools think they got a man and don't even know they ain't got nothin' ... but maybe a hound dog ... snoopin' around the door ... just breath and britches. Even the Bible talks about these kinds of women folk in 2nd Timothy.

Now mind ya, I get a might lonely sometimes since y'alls granddaddy died a good while back, but ain't no man crossin' my threshold if'n I aint heard from God first that he be a *right* Christian man ... and *the* right Christian man just for *me and me alone*.

Well, word come down that big bad Buster had up and died and somebody was gonna hav'ta funeralize his sorry no-count soul. And worser still ... they was gonna have the wake at the Church of the People. We done been funerilizin' folks for as long as I have been goin' to the Church of the People ... and I don't mind tellin' y'all, that's a mighty long time. But I aint never liked the notion of funerializin' folks who aint been saved and sealed and ain't noways no friend of Jesus. If they ain't sealed uptight with the Holy Ghost, all hell mightcould break a'loose. Po' Pastors feel like they gotsta lie about some sorry heathen soul, jesta put 'em in the ground before the stink comes on 'em so strong it drives everybody away. Or maybe them pastors needed to get paid so bad, they was willin' to lie about the man to God Hisself ... for a few measly dollars. Thank the Lord, I don't hav'ta have nothin' to do with sending' somebody off like that ...'cause if'n I was runnin' one of them funerals, I'd have to tell it jes' lack' 'tis ... and let the chips fall where they might ... cause I ain't gonna fall out with Jesus jesta be fibbin' over some sorry, hell-bound heathen soul ... even if'n they paid off the rest of my house note.

Y'all know that right 'cross the road from the Church of the People was the onliest Negro funeral parlor for miles 'round, Terrence Diggs Funeral Parlor and Casket Company ... and right next door was the furniture Store that Mr. Diggs owned too. That is where everybody went to buy phonograph records ... and he sold both kinds ... heavenly records and heathen records. Brother Diggs could bury ya sharp too ... in a beautiful shiny wood casket with brass trimming' or he could bury ya in a driftwood box ... with wormholes already in it. Depends on how much long green you be workin' with and how much of it you want to see buried with your dead kinfolk. Children, I expect y'all to see to it that your Grandmama gets buried simple, cause this ole body ain't nothin' but a loaner ... to get me around until they fit me for my Crown Victoria. Oh Glory!

Chile, all these ne'er do wells was beginnin' to gather for the wake too. You know, nobody wants to miss a free meal ... and if'n you didn't come to the wake *and* the funeral you jus' plain wadn't getting' fed. We could smell that food comin' up from off the little wood stove they had in the church root cellar. Chile, Preachers came from all over the county ... 'cause they never knows when they might git the chance to toss out the Word in front of a big gathering' of folk. Besides, I ain't met a preacher yet, willin' to turn down a free meal.

Just then, Buster's latest, so-called wife showed up ... and right behind her come all these other used-up-lookin' women ... each one draggin' a passel of young'uns behind her. I aint never seed so many stair steps in all my born days ... and I'm gonna figure them stair steps ain't rightly leadin' to the Pearly Gates. Each of them womens was squawkin' and screamin' to high hell ... right there in the Church of the People ...'bout how Buster done promised 'em he was gonna leave 'em a whole bunch of money when he passed. Po' Thangs ... I woulda smelled him a'comin' straight from the get … but they ain't asked the Good Lord God for the power to see mess for what it is. You gotsta have the Holy Ghost to see straight through folks.

Now, the casket, with that ole sorry, no-count behind in it … forgive me Lord … but it was sittin' in the other end of the room closed up with a old yellow stained bedspread over it. Maybe them whinin' womens figured he was scrimpin' on the box, so's he could leave more loot for 'em. Anyways, the box was closed up tight, thank the Good Lord God … 'cause I sho'nuff didn't needta lay eyes on his ugly no count mug again. Then, the latest wife, Ida Dunham, that's Sis. Sadie's wayward chile' … she rose up, clapped her hand real hard five-times-fast and called out to everybody, "Let's just all of us settle down now and show some proper respect for the dead.

As far as I was concerned, he was dead even whilst he was so-called livin' … 'cause he ain't never gave his heart to the Good Lord God … well, at least as far as I know'd in my knower. The preachers was also tryin' to get everybody settled back down right and proper, when, all of a sudden, Deacon Givens come a runnin' in the door shoutin', "dead man or no … he owes me forty dollars and I come to git it." Now Deacon, he liked to play the numbers a little and such … and Buster made a fair livin' at the card table and the pool table. "And besides", Deacon said, "that son of a gun put my wife in a family way ... and I'm gonna need every dime of that money to take care of that new child".

Y'all, I thought I done seen it all, but Brother Givens made a beeline straight for the coffin in the back room ... takin' long strong strides that rattled the floorboards and swingin' his arms back and forth like he was fixin' for a fight ... with a dead man! Lord help 'im. When the Deacon got to the casket, he tossed back the yellow-stained bedspread just like it wadn't nothin' and you could hear the hinges squeakin' whilst he went about openin' up the coffin. Mr. Diggs was tryin' to pull him away and talk some kinda sense into the man. I can understand how he mightcould be peeved, but deacons is s'posta know better than to cause a ruckus up in the church. I s'pose that's what happens when you let a heathen like Buster up in your church ... they gonna stir the devil in folks ... even a dead heathen can drag folks down. Lord, have mercy! I s'pose he was meaning to rummage through Busters buryin' suit just in case there was some money in the pockets. Knowin' Buster, That was a fine suit, too ... and probably paid for by one of them fool gals.

But, instead of hearin' rustlin' and jostlin', we heard loud gigglin' comin' from the casket, like when I tickle one of you young'uns, and Deacon Givens and Bro. Diggs jumped back. Their eyes was bugged out like they just seen a ghost. And just then Buster's dead body sat straight up and the

gigglin' turned into a high-pitch cackle ... like a hyena circlin' a carcass?" Big bad Buster Pride was live as you and
me, and steady cacklin'. Women was clutchin' they hankies
and I was worried that Rev. Dottery mightcould have a con-
niption ... and drop dead his own self ... right there, in the
Church of the People. He wadn't no spring chicken, ya
know!

Sorry children. Lord, please forgive me, but seeing a dead
man walking kinda threw everybody off a little. Then that
heathen started shouting. "I got cha now! Yep! I got all
y'all!" When all the people realized what was going on they
saw that the rascal was not dead after all. I guess he just
wanted to see what people was gonna say 'bout him after he
was dead and gone. Lotsa folk wonder on foolishness like
that, but you best be concerned 'bout what the Good Lord
God gonna say ... not a bunch of heathen heifers.

By this time, everybody in the church had jumped up
running over each other just trying to get out of the Church
of the People. Bad ole Buster just kept cacklin' and shoutin', "I gotcha! I gotch'all! Buster musta thunk this was like
a dress rehearsal for his real funeral. Fact is children, our
whole lives ain't nothin' but a dress rehearsal for our time
with the Good Lord God ... and if'n we choose to do right
by folks and study and pray like the Good Book say, you
won't have to deal with the likes of Buster in the sweet by

and by. Ole Buster's punched his ticket for a southbound express, where there ain't no rest.

Well, it wadn't no wake like I ever heard of or seen … before or since … but I guess that wake done woked up some of those po' womens who fell for Busters sweet line o'jive, 'cause years later, when he done died fo' real, wadn't nary a soul showed up … and none showed-out neither … no weepin' or moanin' … no passel of stair steps or womens arguin' 'bout Busters money. Now that's what I call a "good" bye, 'cause where he be's goin', wadn't nobody wanted to go with him … and that's how it should be.

Children, you gonna meet plenty folks in this crazy world claimin' to be a Child of the Good Lord God … just cause it sounds good to say it and it feels good to em' to believe it. But, the Holy Spirit that lives inside of each believer is gonna tell ya true who is a child of God and who aint … no matter what they might say to make you think elsewise. 'Cause there's a thin line between Heaven and Hell, and that's something only the Holy Spirit can tell.

THE QUALITY OF PERCY and THE QUANTITY OF MERCY

Dear friends, let us love one another, for love comes from God. Everyone who loves has been born of God and knows God.

1st John 4:7

Children, I want you younger ones to go on out and play for a while so's I can talk to the older children about something serious ... something that people don't much like talkin' about.

Now children, have you ever heard anybody call somebody else a sissy? Well, it just ain't right to call people nasty names 'cause you don't like something you *think* you know about 'em. It takes all kinda people to make up this crazy world and the last thing Negroes need to be doin' is puttin' folks down like we been put down. I been livin' in this crazy world a good long time and it still hurts when people use nasty names on us, so, I won't abide any such mess from nobody … especially *my* grands. If I ever hear about any of you talkin' about sissies or faggots or queers, I'm sho 'nuff going get out the old splintered up board of education that hangs on the hook in the kitchen and apply it long and hard to your sorry seats of learning. If you don't get what I mean … I'll whoop ya but good … and if'n ya think your hind parts ain't sorry, you tell me how sorry they be after I'm finished wailin' on 'em. Name callin' don't please the Good Lord God and judgin' folks you don't really know don't much please me.

I'll tell ya why I picked this time to talk to you about it. Ya see, Mr. Percy had to leave the church 'cause folks was treatin' him so bad … well, not all folks … but mostly Elder Stoneham's only child, Tobias … You know, that big strappin' boy everybody calls Toba. He thinks 'cause his daddy owns all those dry cleanin' stores and got made church elder, that he can act jes' any kinda way with any ole body. I don't care who his daddy is, that is one nasty little demon. Yeah, you heard me right. Any right child of the Good Lord God that don't recognize a demon when he shows hisself, ain't got no Holy Spirit nohow. Besides, I don't need no dry-cleanin'. I can wash and press my own things and I ain't likely to throw my little bit of money away paying for something I can sho 'nuff do my own self. I ain't no ways lazy … nor foolish with my money neither. It don't take no genius see that Toba thinks mighty highly of hisself, what with being captain of the football team last year and havin' all those fancy clothes he got with daddy's money and havin' that cement swimmin' hole in his back yard. I'm guessin' you young folks mightcould fall for all that stuff. Believe me, if he didn't earn it hisself, it ain't his boast to boast about or get puffed up over.

But, Lord knows this thing with Percy done really got me sad in my spirit. It's a shame too, 'cause Percy Lee Cane is a good man and a good friend … it's just that he has some ways about him that ain't quite right. But Percy Lee is as nice a person as you'd ever wanna meet … and he would never say or do nothing to hurt nobody. But, like all of us, he's got a ways to go to get right with God … and God's surely workin' on him … just like He's workin' on all the rest of us. But the thorn in Percy's side is a little different than most folks. The Good Lord God knows it … and He understands it … and he's surely gonna work it out right for Percy, just like he doing with all his children …'cause old Percy is a child of the Good Lord God … and God don't make no junk … not me … not you … not Percy too.

Now, I've been knowin' Percy since he was a young boy, and he was different even then, but always sweet and nice and ready to do somethin' nice for everybody he knew. Heck, when I was in the hospital back when ... with my rheumatism, Percy come over every few days to mow my grass and clean off my porch. I know I don't have no big yard and it ain't no major chore, but no other body else offered but Percy, and I was tickled pink to have his help. He did a fine job too! And when I tried to offer him a few little dollars he wouldn't take it. I was really thankful for that too ... 'cause that's what right Christian's do for one 'nother. It's a fact that nobody ever seen him goin' out with the ladies, but he don't drink nor smoke neither. He's a good man ... but quirky in a way that ain't quite right.

I believe in my spirit that his odd ways started when he was real young and his mama just kept him tied to her apron string day and night. He didn't have no daddy around most of his life. His poor mama married a man for a short while when Percy was about 12 or so, but he used to beat 'em both so bad, she had to call the law on him and ain't nobody seen that demon since, thank you. God don't want us to sit still and let evil folk have their way. They say he'd been in jail a bunch of times before that and likely learned some mighty evil ways in there. Word was, he used to jump little Percy in unnatural ways and beat him with no mercy.

But even through it all, Percy stayed beautiful in his heart to everyone around him. Heaven knows he coulda been somethin' terrible if the Good Lord God hadn'ta kept him. Pain and hurt can make folks do crazy things ... hurtful things. Fact is, most folks that been through the kinda sufferin' Percy been through, either wastes their lives hurtin' people or hurtin' theyselves. Percy never hurt nobody ... 'cept maybe Percy.

Well, after livin' quietly in his odd ways about thirty years or so, he came to talk to me and told me some things about his life that surely wasn't right, but wasn't no worser than most of us when we get caught up in our *real* mess. I'm not talkin' bout these mush-mouth churchy folks who get up every Sunday to testify ... more like test-a-lie. Yeah you heard me ... and even I wadn't always a perfect saint ... matter of fact, I ain't all the way there yet, but I guess that's a good thing ...'cause if'n I was, the Good Lord God would be callin' me on home ... and you kids still need your old granny, to learn ya the Good Lord God's ways, don't ya? Well, don't ya? Well ... alright then!

Anyhow, after Percy talked to me I told him he oughta talk to Pastor right away to figure out what to do about the things that was troublin' him, while the Holy Spirit was movin' on him. Problem is, I didn't know Pastor was fixin' to head outta town with his family for a few days ... and Pastor must not have know'd just what was troublin' Percy neither when Percy asked to talk with him. Now, Pastor is a fine and thoughtful man of God, but not knowin' the nature of Percy's need, he just told Percy to take it up with Elder Stoneham.

I gotta tell ya children, Elder Curtis Stoneham wouldn'ta been my first choice for elder at *my* church. He got a kinda self-satisfied way about him that rubs me wrong ... and he so big and gruff in his ways. Yeah, he's studied his Bible good enough, but I gotta wonder if he ever set his own self aside long enough to let the Holy Spirit have *His* way. I suppose owning five dry cleanin' stores in the county makes him a good tither ... you know, Curt's Cleaners, and in most churches, a good tither seems to find his way to the top of the peckin' order in church ... in short order. It's just that Elder Stoneham wouldn'ta been my first choice ... or second ... or fifth, for that matter. I believe elder had a thing or three to learn about humbleness. But that's who Percy ended up pullin' aside when it came time to lay hisself bare and surrender his earthly sin to the Good Lord God. Have mercy!

Mind you, some folks who have odd ways like Percy will set upon young children to do their mess with ... and if I ever heard that Percy Lee Cane touched one nappy little hair on the head of one nappy little child in this whole darn county, I'd go straight after him ... friend or no. You know that big cleaver I got that I use when we barbecue the whole hog. I'd have to introduce old Percy to U.S. Steel ... it can cut up vitals just as good as vittles ... and his vitals would be on the firin' line. I wouldn't even care what happen to me. I'd haveta just start prunin' his parts and let the chips fall where they might. But, thank God, Percy wasn't that kinda way. Problem is, Elder Stoneham could cut ya like a knife without even knowin' it, just by being his own self-righteous self. Poor Percy!

He came to see me afterward cryin' like a baby ... said he ain't been hurt so hard since his step-daddy left.

Next thing ya know, Toba starts in tauntin' Percy without mercy. His loud-talkin' daddy musta said somethin' loud enough that let Toba know what was up with Percy and 'fore long the whole dang town was privy to it. Most of 'em probably had an inklin' 'bout Percy, but when a child of God confesses and submits his sin to the Good Lord God's correctin' ways, he shouldn't hav'ta let the whole town know about his mess. You know children, if walls could talk about what all they hear, wouldn't nobody say a mumblin' word about Percy ... or nobody else for that matter. But, I guess the damage was done, 'cause Percy was sho' nuff hurtin' fo' certain. I hugged him and prayed my little heart out for him. I wish I knew what the Good Lord God was thinkin' when he let Pastor leave town ... just when Percy was ready to let the Holy Spirit move on him to change his odd ways. Lord, have mercy on Mr. Percy! Fact is, if we keep treatin' folks the way Percy got treated, nobody's ever gonna come to the Good Lord God to confess their sin no more ... and before ya know it, folks with odd ways like Percy be leadin' the choir or even preachin' the Word. Lord, help us!

Children, you need to *know* ... that sin is sin is sin. Ain't no good sin or better sin, when it's sin that you're in. Some folks would have you think that sin was like a poker game ... where a straight beats two of a kind and sex sin trumps murder. Fact is, ain't no more or less sin ... it's all a mess sin ... and that's how the Bible tells it. The only sin we got *any* right to judge is our *own* sin. Anybody's else's gotta go up for God ... and God alone to judge. Always remember this. The only sin that got ole Satan booted outta heaven was the sin of bein' so self-satisfied that he thought he could do God's job, and there ain't hardly no sin no worser than that!

Anyway, we didn't see hide nor hair of Percy for a good long time ... and I truly missed his sweet smile and gentle ways. Then one day about six months later the whole town was in a tizzy. Seems that the law caught that demon Toba with his nasty paws in some little girl's honey pot ... and she wasn't but thirteen years old. Toba musta been about 19 ... and like they say, 13 will sho' nuff get ya 20 ... in jail. I never seed Elder Stoneham so quiet and sunken over in sadness. Just like with Percy, when news travels in a small town, everybody gets wind of it in about two seconds flat ... and Elder was feeling mighty small ... or at least wishin' he could shrink up and disappear. But he was a big shot business man and an elder ... and folks expect a lot from folks when they set themselves up as knowin' what's best for everybody ... everybody but their own, that is.

I guess I felt a little piece of pity for the man too. After all, the Good Book says that we all bound to fall short of the Good Lord God's perfect glory. That old Prophet musta seen Elder and Toba a comin', when the Holy Spirit had him to write that piece in the Book. Well, that next Sunday, after Pastor had got back from his trip, the feelin' in the church service was lower than low. The singers wasn't rightly feelin' the Spirit. Nobody was shoutin' "amen!" or speakin' in tongues. It didn't really feel like church at all, children. Everybody looked like zombies ... just a trudgin' through the motions. Finally, Pastor got up to preach and he just stood there ... for the longest time. The quiet was so loud it like to scare me, and we wasn't sure he was ever gonna speak. Then he slowly reached into his jacket pocket and pulled out a wrinkled up, folded up piece of paper that looked like it had some water stains on it. He slowly unfolded it and pulled out his wire frame specs. Then, he pulled out his hanky and slowly unfolded it and wiped off his specs. Then he took the hanky and rubbed his eyes for a good long time before he wrapped the specs 'round his ears and began to read:

> Dear Pastor
> I heard the news about Toba and a sadness hit my soul so hard I just had to write you. Please have the People in the church, and your own self, of course, pray for Toba … and for Elder and his whole family. Our God is surely a God of mercy. He's been so merciful to me and he'll surely have mercy on Toba too, 'cause this is a good church, with good People … that honor the Good Lord God. Please tell Elder I be prayin' for him every day … just like I *know*, he been prayin' for me. Sometimes, things happens to us that hurt so hard, that we Can't seem to find any feelings left … or even the will justa pray … and that's when the devil takes *his* chance to have *his* own way. Just keep prayin' for him, Pastor … and pray for me too.
> Fondly,
> Percy Lee Cane, Child of the Good Lord God

Well, that worry-weary church started to wake up all of a sudden and you could hear the sweet sound of folks sendin' up their spirits sayin, "Hallelujah!" and "Praise Him! and "Thank you Jesus!" and "Glory to His name!" and "Amen!". Just that sudden, *my* church was back to bein' *my* church again … and it felt *so* good. And children, Percy wrote me a letter too … that he was comin' back to town. Prayer really works …'cause that good-news letter was an answer to one of *my* prayers. Thank ya Lord!!

Then Pastor asked the choir to sing, "I Surrender All" and the service ended right there. We didn't need no sermon. You see, sometimes when the Holy Spirit makes *His* move on *His* church People, ain't no need for no program to guide the order in the service, just so long as we remember who the service be servin'. Amen? … Amen!

Note: The Hebrew word "Toebah" translates to abominable, detestable, vile. In the original Hebrew, the word "Toebah" was applied to virtually every sin mentioned in the Old Testament. However, in the English translation the word abomination was applied to homosexuality only. This has enabled homophobes within church leadership to rail self-righteously that homosexuality is more sinful than other sins. However, the sin that is cited most often in scripture is

Satan's sins … that of self-sufficiency and arrogance.

THE ANNUAL
CHURCH FOOT
WASHIN'

Jesus spoke, "The greatest among you will be your ser-
vant. For whoever exalts himself will be humbled, and
whoever humbles himself will be exalted."

Matthew 23:12

Let me tell ya somethin', in life you are bound to meet up
with folks or come in contact with people with all kinds of
afflictions. What is a affliction? Y'all don't know what that
is? Well, it's like a sickness on some part of your body. You
ever seen somebody with cross-eyes? Or somebody with
bowlegs, those is afflictions. And pert near every part of the
body, can be afflicted

The Good Lord God don't look down on nobody jes'
'cause of some affliction they may have got. You know,
Negroes have been 'buked and scorned for a long, long

time. I hear tell from my Grandmama 'bout people with welts on their backs stickin way out where the slave masters done beat 'em with a whip. Yes chile, we done had more than our fare share of afflictions … of every and all kinds … and there aint near no part of the body that can't be afflicted … from the crown of your head to the soles of your feet.

But Jesus was sent here to heal all of our afflictions; He is the Balm of Gilead; the doctor in the sick room; a rock in the soul; healer of lepers and the downhearted soul. Yes, Jesus has been with us a mighty long time … and he knows what being beat with a whip is all about.

Even the best upright Christians have thorns in the flesh … and what I mean by that is … we got things about us that done causes us to fall short of God's glory … but we still know that if we have the Good Lord God on our side, that he loves us thorns and all … and that, my children, is a soothin' thing to know in your heart.

And just like Jesus loves us even with our afflictions and our thorns and our mess, we s'posta love one another's thorns and all … afflictions and all … and that is what being a right good Christian is all about.

Do y'all know that Jesus, the King of Kings and Lord of Lords, even washed his disciples feet … you know … the folk that followed behind Jesus everywhere he went, so's they could learn about the right ways a Christian s'posta be and the power of the Holy Ghost to heal every affliction know'd to man. All through the Bible, they was telling stories about Jesus healin' this one and that one. Oh Glory! I thank you Lord!! I remember in the Bible where Jesus helped a man to walk who couldn't walk since he was born.

You know, in this country we got ourselves a president … and thank the Good Lord God, we change him up every four years or so … 'cause aint nary one of 'em worth a hoot or holler to Negro folks. But if you go over to those countries across the ocean where the white folks come from, they all got Kings … and you can bet your last penny ain't none of them kings kneelln' down to wash nobody's stanky feet … But ***JESUS, THE KING OF KINGS*** washed all the feet of the folks that followed 'round behind Him.

Aint nobody too good to kneel down and wash some strangers feet 'cause we was put here by the Good Lord God to serve … not to be served. That's how Jesus done told us to do it in the Bible.

Chile, let me tell y'all somethin'. It's about the last annual foot washin'. You see, church folks liked to do things like Jesus done 'em and so that's why we make a special day out of the annual foot washin'. But after I tell y'all this story you will know why we don't do foot washin' no more … 'cause the Good Lord God won't give you more than you can bear

... and speakin' for myself ... and everybody else at the Church of the People ... that was one burden too many. Forgive me Lord, but we all fall short of what you want us to do ... even Grandmama sometimes.

Don't y'all know that we was all at the church gathrin' to get ready for the annual foot washin. Sister Tawana K. Tubbs, she used to take in white folks laundry to wash in her basin out on her back porch and she done dragged the basin with her all the ways to church, ... so's we could wash feet in the basin. May The Good Lord God bless her. We knew we was gonna need a lot of soap cause us country folk walk around without our shoes a lot. So we asked Brother Clyde Toombs, who works at the prison up the road in Freetown, to bring a big case of lye soap.

They tell me that everybody that comes into prison gotta be scrubbed down real good with lye soap, 'cause it kills lice, bed bugs, ticks, fleas, chiggers ... stop gigglin' ... I said chiggers with a c ... and anything that mightcoulda hitched a ride in on some heathen, jailbird's unwashed body.

We asked Elder Brooms to bring a whole heap of towels. You see, he works as a janitor at the big Veterans Hospital up in Jeffersonville. Lord, I sho' hope Elder didn't lift them towels ... if you know what I mean ... cause there must have been at least fifty of em. We had Sister Rosemary Gardner bring a great big old rolled up lawn hose, so's we could hitch it up behind the back of the church and bring it in the side window to fill up the basin. Sister Rosemary's husband Woody had his own lawn mowin' business and he let us borrow his hose.

Chile, when we went to unroll the hose we saw all kinds of patches, tape, string, chewin' gum and rubber bands wrapped around it ... but the bucket brigade at the firehouse was not available ... and Grandmama was not gonna be haulin' water hither and yon. That just wasn't gonna happen.

Now, everybody in the Church of The People was gonna take turns getting they feets washed and washin' somebody else's feets. Problem was, nobody wanted to be first. They didn't want to be the first to bear their soles, I guess. But I leaned over to Sister Gladys Cornwell and told her softly if she didn't get ta steppin' over to that basin, I was gonna let all her stuff be know'd. Forgive me Lord, somebody had to be first, and it wasn't gonna be me. I gladly volunteered to wash feet, I'm use'ta doing that ... what with all the years of washin' you little hellions feets ... trust me, I have washed many of crusty little and big foot and everything else ... so washin feets don't bother me none ... or so I thought. Mind y'all, it was only three of us in charge of all the washin'.

Chile, when Sister Cornwell took off her shoes, took off her socks and wouldn't you know she had the ugliest hammertoes I's ever seen. Y'all know what a hammertoe is? It looks like Grandmama's garden hoe. The tops of her toes was all stuck upwards ... and the ends was all turned under. That makes me believe that she can't be a right walkin' Christian with feet like that. Chile, I had to close my eyes and pray as I washed 'em, 'cause Lord knows, I couldn't look at 'em. Ooh, I was so glad that my turn to wash feet was over after that awful mess. Chile, now I *really* know what trials and tribulations is all about. I hope to God that the disciples' feets never looked like that!

Next to get his feets washed was Elder Broome. He took off his broghans shoes and his argyle socks and wouldn't you know it ... two of his little toes on his right foot was missin'. God bless him, the Good Lord knows ... that when we walk with Jesus we will not be de-feeted. And like as if that wasn't 'nuff, the toes that was left had toenails that must have been a half-inch thick. You would need a hacksaw to trim them nails. I've heard that a lot of the menfolk come back from the war with trench foot ... and they toes get like that. Now Lord knows I loved my husband while he was here, but if he ever introduced toes like that to my good bedsheets, he'd sho'nuff be sleepin' on the couch.

Next to get her feet washed was sweet, humble Sister Bernadette Neelon. We all looked at her with great pity cause she looked so homely, but she was so nice to everybody. She was a scrub woman ... spend most of her life down on her knees scrubbin' folks floors, outhouses, bathtubs and the like ... all the things other people tries to git outta doin' if they could. When she took off her shoes I was mighty hurt to see the sad condition of her tired little dogs. Chile, I saw blisters, calluses, bunions, corns ... and if that wasn't bad enough she had ingrown toenails that was hurtin me to look at ... and I know it had to be hurtin her ... po' thang.

I noticed that she looked a might shamed 'cause of showin' her feet to all of us. But as she allowed herself to dip 'em down into the water ... and let somebody begin to touch her feet and softly wash them, she began to slowly change the shamed look on her face. It was nice to see her begin to smile and whisper with contentment, "Thank you Jesus, thank you Jesus. I was sure from the look on her face that it felt mighty good to be touched by one of the saints ... put the shoe on the other foot ... so to speak.

All the while, each member was getting they feets washed, the pastor was praying over them and said over and over that he wanted to be last, just like the Bible says Jesus done. After washin' those nasty afflicted looking feet I just felt like I had to go and wash my hands again, but I didn't want nobody to notice ... didn't want them to think I thought I was too good to wash somebody's feet. So I eased out the back door kinda quiet like. You know the outhouse is jes five steps from the front door and I washed my hands two or three times before I came back in.

Chile, timin' is everything. Let me tell y'all what I mean. Just like the gospel song says, I come in the back door and somethin hit me like a atom bomb. It was the stankiest stench my nose ever smelt. Chile, the Good Lord God gave us Negroes special noses … wide and beautiful with big nostrils so's we could hum real sweet and sing real strong. Now, I never wished for nothin about me to be like white folks, but as God is my witness, if I coulda had one of those little tight-holed skinny white folks noses, it sure would have been a blessin' right then and there.

The smell that come up in my nostrils … I just hadta pray it was gonna leave some time soon.

Lord, have mercy. I just went out to wash my hands … didn't want nobody to know … but s'posin' they might think that skank be coming from the outhouse I just left. As God is my witness, last night I didn't have no collards, no okra, no chittlins, cabbage … none of that stuff that might-could cause that kind of a stink … if'n you know what I mean.

Chile, I stepped back into the church and was mighty relieved that wasn't nobody worryin 'bout what I ate last night … cause it was for sure that the stink was comin from the church … and the onliest one with they shoes off was our Pastor, Reverend Elmo P. Goodfoot … and trust me there was nothin' good about it!

I couldn't believe the odor was coming from the Pastor, cause he was the most fine, handsome, tall, refined Negro man I had ever seen. We all looked at each other with the strangest expressions on our faces ... cheeks all puffed out like Dizzy Gillespie ... 'cause we could hardly breathe. Chile, before I knew it, folks was pulling towels left and right to cover they mouths and noses. You never seen Grandmama move so fast to get me a towel before they were all gone. Lord Knows, I thought I would fall out on the floor. Forgive me for complainin' 'bout havin' to wash that clawfoot tub ...'cause you saved me,

Lord ... from havin' to touch Pastor's foot ...'cause you know Lord ... it done stunk to high hell. Matter of fact, Lord, you picked the right one to wash the pastor's feets. While the rest of us was cringing and cowwerin' and tryin' to ease away from the wash basin without nobody noticing, Sister Bernadette was lovingly washin' pastors feet without fuss or murmur ... that was just her way.

Thank the Good Lord God ... whilst we was all scramblin' for towels to cover our faces, there was at least two towels left. One for pastor to dry his wet feet, after which he might thankfully put his shoes and socks back on ... and I hope I never have to witness him putting his shoes back on ever again. The last towel was for Sister Bernadette to wipe off her hands.

The main reason I am tellin' y'all this story is cause I would sooner you face hard times in life with a humble spirit like Sister Bernadette, then do like your Grandmama done … just lookin' out for your own self and worrin' about what other folk think. We don't know what Jesus might have seen or smelled or had to deal with when He kneeled down to wash the feet of His disciples, but I know He did it humbly and with love … and to show everyone … aint nobody too good to do life's dirty work. Remember, y'all, only what we do for Christ Jesus will last! He gives rewards to any task he assigns.

THE ANNUAL
CHURCH BAKE SALE

Pride goes before destruction, a haughty spirit before a fall.

Proverbs 16:18

Now, you older young'uns can go 'bout your chores 'cause I got a special story to tell the sugar-sugars ... my little baby grands, 'bout the big Bake Sale contest ... and Grandmama wanted to win that contest in the worst way ... and that pretty much describes how I went 'bout it too ... in the worst way! Chile, this is something that I am almost ashamed to tell y'all cause I lost my Christian rightness trying to become the winner of the annual congregation bake sale and contest.

"What do you mean Grandmama?"

Chile, I broke at least three of the Good Lord God's commandments. First, I stole a recipe from my next-door neighbor Maxine Flatface. Then I lied to the president of the Bake Club at the church by telling her that I had never baked the cake that I ended up baking. And last, I coveted Sister Shocancook's special cookbook, since I didn't think that I could win the contest any other way. But not only did I do what I just told y'all, I even did something else more devious.

"What did you do Grandmama?"

Chile, when I was taking the first layers of the cake out of the oven ... Oh! I forgot to tell y'all what kind of cake I baked ... I baked a Sockittome Cake. Anyway, as I was taking it out of the oven, it fell on the kitchen floor, and I accidentally stepped on it. What a mess ... the thick wool sock that I had on my left foot got stuck in the cake, and I could not get it out, so I just left it in there. I tried real hard to get it out, but I couldn't ... not without spoilin' the whole dang thang. So like I said, I left it in there.

Anyway, I knew that I was getting sleepy cause I hadn't really had any sleep. I was so sleepy that I forgot to put the eggs in the cake, so I waited for the cake to cool down and put five eggs right in the middle of the cake.

"Do you mean that you put eggs still in their shells in the cake, Grandmama?" "Yes, I did," answered Grandmama. Truly, I was so caught up in making sure that I made the best cake, I didn't care what I had to do to make it happen. I guess I wanted to win so bad 'cause I entered the annual bake sale and contest ten straight years ... and had never won. And everybody in the county knows your Grand-mama can sho'nuff throw down in the kitchen ... that means I can cook good ... right? Dern tootin'!

I tell y'all, my conscience started bothering me minute-by-minute, especially when I took the second and third layers out of the oven.

"Why, Grandmama?"

Well, when I took out those layers, I remembered that I forgot to add the milk that the cow had worked so hard to give me for the cake. So, I just waited for the cake to cool down and poured some milk into the middle of all four layers, including the layer that had the thick wool sock stuck in it. I know what y'all might be thinking about me by now, but I told y'all I was ashamed to tell you this story in the first place.

Now, I knew that I had a slim chance to win cause Sister Shocancook said that she was going to enter the bake sale and contest, and everybody in the county knew that she was the best baker 100 miles 'round this whole area. So I thought about bakin' a cake that folks wouldn't never forget. Yes, I sure made sure that the will of the Good Lord God was in my favor ... at least so far as the bake sale was concerned.

Well, I was in my kitchen on the day of the bake sale early that morning ... I guess it was about four o'clock. I remember I was half sleep 'cause Sadie's cow had me up all night trying to help her have her calf, and she was up all night trying to help me ... by giving me some fresh milk for the cake.

Later in the day, after I found the powdered sugar I'd hid under the porch ten years ago, I made the frostin' for the cake. It looked real good when I finished too, 'cause you couldn't see the sock, the five eggs, and the milk that I had put in after the cake's layers had already been baked. So, like I said, I frosted the cake, and ... if'n I say so myself ... it sho' 'nuff *looked* good. I can't say how it tasted 'cause I didn't taste it. I knew that if I ate any, folks might not wanna buy it. Or the judges might see that it weren't quite perfect and toss me out the contest.

When it was time to take the cakes to the Church of the People, I got down on my knees and asked the Good Lord God to forgive me for breakin' his commandments in making the Sockittome Cake. I *think* I heard the Good Lord God say something to me ... but his voice was too low, so I wasn't really sure what the Good Lord God said.

I hauled my Sockittome Cake on over to the fair ... and set it up nice ... right 'tween Mrs. Nutbush's pecan cream cake and Sis. Skinnyminnie's pound cake ... on the long wooden table covered with the purple and orange tablecloth. Then, I heard somebody talkin' 'bout Sister Shocancook.

"Chile, I hear she done come down with the flu and didn't feel up to stayin' wake last night bakin' nothin'. Po' thang won't be entering no thang in the contest this year."

When I heard that, I fell to my knees and begged God not to let nobody buy my cake before the judges had a chance to see it.

Well, I believe that the Good Lord God heard my prayer, 'cause I heard one of the judges' say, "We are commencin' the judgin' of the baked goods at this time. Would everyone please surround the table so that we can test the baked goods and make a decision on the first, second, and third place winners? Chile, when I heard the judge say that, I wanted to drop through the floor "cause I didn't want nobody to eat my cake. After all, there was a sho'nuff sock in my Sockittome Cake.

My Lord, y'all won't believe what happened. The judges tasted about nine baked pies and eleven cakes, and then they got to mine. When the first judge placed the knife into the cake, I dropped my head and started praying again. But the Good Lord God still had not spoken loud enough for me to hear what he had to tell me … so I just kept my head down.

All of a sudden, I heard the voice of one of the judges start to shout to the other judges, "Y'all have to eat this Sockittome Cake 'cause it's the best thing on the table. I'll tell y'all … somebody sho'nuff put they foot in this cake. I have never had a cake taste this good in all my life," said the judge.

I suppose by now you realize that I won first place … Oh! I also heard loud and clear from the Good Lord God. He told me that He heard me, but that He was giving me a chance to repent and remove that cake before somebody ate some of it. But, he said, since I truly didn't hear him very good at first, that he just flipped the whole thang 'round for any folks that tried my cake. Do you know what the Good Lord God did for me without me realizing it? He removed the sock and put the eggs and the milk in the places they was s'poseda be…. And that's why the judge liked my cake so darn much … the Sockittome Cake *without* the sock.

Grandmama smiled as she told us this part of the story. "Now, you tell me," said Grandmama, "the Good Lord God is just awesome … ain't He? He saved me from my own self. I never entered another bake sale or contest after that!"

THE PEOPLE'S 10TH YEAR ANNUAL FASHION SHOW

All a man's ways seem innocent to him, but the Lord weighs motives.

Proverbs 16:2

Now, you older young'uns might just so well run on and play ...'cause the story I got today is special ... for the little ones ... that ain't so ready as you older young'uns to poo-poo everything Grandmama done told 'em. So, this one's for the sugar-sugars.

Now, we had all sizes of womenfolk and menfolk in our church. And the fashion show was for grownfolks only or else us grown ladies wouldn't never've had a chance in China ...'cause them young gals are built up ... like a Coca

Cola bottle. And trust me, I ain't seen my waist since General Lee and General Grant had that big fight down yonder ways. Anyway Chile, I didn't know right away what I wanted to wear cause I had to give some good mind to what done happened to this ole body of mine over the years.

"What do you mean, Grandmama?"

Chile … I can walk ya thru all the changes of life this old bag o' bones been thru:

I do recall that when I was 5 years old, I could take my legs … and twist 'em 'round my neck … and still have room to raise 'em up even higher.

And in the first grade, I could swing on the monkey bars behind the school and hang there for a long, long time …

Second grade, I could run faster than anybody in my class. In fact, they started into callin' me *the tornado,* 'cause that's how fast I'd run. All though my school years, I run on the track team agin' kids from twenty different districts.

I could kick a ball farther even than my big brother, Boots. Chile, don't y'all know there was nobody who could kick a ball like me?

Anyway, I began to realize that I had springs in my knees … so I decided to go out for high jump … and believe you me, y'all, I was the best jumper for seven cities 'round.

When I went to the tenth grade the teachers all told me that I had the mind of a genius and that I could out-argue anybody, including the devil, hisself … so I went out for the de-bate team.

And in twefth grade, I knew it was my last chance to play basketball, so I tried out for the team. Trust me, everybody said that I played better than the ones on my team … and the ones on the other team combined. Well, I suppose that is the gist of my physical gifts from back when I was a young gal.

From the age of eighteen through the age of twenty-five, I was the best dancer at the Young People's Last Chance to Dance Club … over in Hicksville. And, when I reached my thirty-second birthday, I started to notice that I could not move like I once did, especially when I went out to dance on the weekends. So, I decided that maybe I would start slowing down and start doing other things with this body of mine.

"What did you start doing, Grandmama?"

Chile, I started doing laundry for people in the nearby town. I figured that I could iron at my own pace and not worry 'bout how fast I was doing it neither. From age thirty-six to age fifty, I started taking evenin' strolls … with the other gettin' older folk in the area. Matter of fact, that's when I met my best friend, Irene Strode. Chile, that woman knows she could walk. One day she walked me 'cross three county lines. I was so tired that my feet had to grow two more toes … jesta keep me from falling … and just so that I could make it back home without fallin' out right on the side of the road. After that I told Irene that she would hav'ta go walkin' by her own self next time and not to never ask me to go walking with her again.

Between the ages of fifty and seventy, I decided to join the Christian Sisters Auxillory Support Group … and I started reaching' out to help those folks that didn't have as much as some. You see, the church was the onliest place to go to get help … for young mamas havin' they first babies … and the daddies weren't nowhere to be found … for whatever reason. I liked doing that cause it reminded me of y'all's Aunt Verdie Mae. She had two babies and no daddies … and believe you me, that was some kinda hard on her. So, I helped her with the babies. Now you can see that over the years this po' bag o' bones done slowed down a dab, and, I 'spose I look like it.

I guess you all might be wondering what I did from the age of seventy-one until now. Well, I don't quite remember 'cause my mind done begun to slow down a might. Anyways, I know some things won't change, and that is my love for you sweet baby grands. I will never let my mind slip so far so's to forget my babies. Y'all will always be my babies, and I don't feel like I am a Grandmama to y'all. No, I feel like a real Mama … cause that's how close my heart is tied up in you.

Well, back to what I wore to the fashion show:

My yellow Roarin' 20's dress with the long squirrel fur wrap 'round the neck and my short green and yellow wool socks … struttin' down the runway. Oh! I forgot about the shoes. Chile, I wore my patent leather open-toe, tie-up orthopedic shoes with the three-inch heels and my red-striped stockings. Oops! … almost forgot the jewelry. I put on my beautiful purple pearls with a rhinestone bracelet and my two-inch wide birthstone ring. Yes, that is exactly what I had a mind to wear. That was one heckuva combo, and nobody could tell me that I wadn't the best dressed woman coming out the shoot.

"Grandmama … if it was summertime, how come you was wearin' all that hot stuff on?"

Chile, I done told y'all that getting' older means every-thing on this old body done changed, and that includes my body heat too!

The big Fashion Show was about to begin, so I went 'round to the back to start getting dressed … when my right eye wandered over to Sara Jeanette. She was pulling some old rags out of her bags, and I just had to see what she was getting out of themthere bags … and when I saw what it was, I coulda hit the floor flat out in shock.

"Whadduya mean, Grandmama?"

Chile, that woman had the nerve to have the same outfit and the same jewelry as me for the big event. I went over to where she was standing and asked her what she was doin'.

She asked me what was I talking about, so I showed her my outfit and my jewelry, and she said, "Well, what do you expect *me* to do about it?" I told her that she was not going to wear that outfit cause she would make me look bad ...'cause she weighed about 75 pounds with legs that looked like pencils.... and that she might s'well put them rags back in them bags and head on home. All of a sudden, she reached her broom-handle left arm back ... with all the might she could muster ... and slapped me right smack 'cross my face. Lord, Chile, it was on ...'cause everybody knows ... I ain't the one!

Now I done told y'all that my body done slowed down since I started reachin' the age of seventy. But before I knew I done it ... I done kicked her bony buttocks all the way 'cross the runway to the other side of the pallet stage ... where everybody was waiting for the models to come out. As she went a flyin' through the air, the people started runnin' and screamin', 'cause they done heard all the commotion ... and done seen Sara Jeanette flying away like she was heaven bound ... even though hell might be closer to it!

But, like I said, in my early days I *was* the best kickball player, and I guess there are some things your body don't forget how to do ... like how to ride a bike.

After the commotion done died down, I realized what I had done and fell down on my knees to ask the Good Lord God to forgive me ...'cause ... after all ... we was scrappin' in the Lord's house. To be honest, I really didn't wanna really repent, but I knew that if I didn't God would not hear me when I prayed to him to help my vegetables grow in my garden behind the house. Well, children, the day ended without us having the fashion show after all … all cause all the models done run away after the big commotion. And there weren't no audience neither … to clap their votes for us. I guess some things just ain't meant to turn out the way we plan …'specially if somethin' happens like that stunt Sara Jeanette pulled. You see, none of that mess would have gotten started in the first place if she had just put those rags of hers back in those bags of hers … like I asked … and they wouldn'ta called the whole thang off. No, I guess things don't always turn out like you would want them … do they?

"No, Grandmama!"

Now, you children are young … like I was once. What are you gonna be great at doin'?..not just good … but great … the best! Don't never settle for bein' jes' so-so at doin' something … don't matter whether it be somethin' you likes to do … or somethin' you gots to do. Always do the very best you can do … and be the very best you can be. The Good Lord God only wants the best for ya … and He 'spects the best from ya too!

Grandmama ain't enterin' no more Fashion Contests. It's just way too temptin' for my weak side. Grandmama hopes you babies can learn from my misdoin's.

THE HOLY WINE HEIST

Give beer to those who are perishing, wine to those who are in anguish; let them drink and forget their poverty. And remember their misery no more.

Proverbs 31:6

The next story Grandmama told us was about the Holy Wine Heist at the Church of the People. She said that the day started out just wonderful it seemed. And we asked her what did she mean by it seem like everything was wonderful?

"You always say that, Grandmama".

Chile, I'm a gonna tell you all something that I don't think you'll never forget. It happened one Sunday morning whilst it was rainin' cats and dogs outside. At first, when I got out of bed, I said to myself, "self, let's not go to church today. It's too darn rainy and nasty out there." But self said, "you know we can't miss church this morning ... 'cause, who's gonna sit on the next to the last pew to examine what everybody be wearin' and what kind of spirit they be totin' into the House of the Good Lord God." So, after listening to myself, I decided I had better get my own self dressed and head on off to the House of the Good Lord God … even if it was rainin' like all get out outside.

Now, I was walking to the church and I noticed the neighborhood wine-o leanin' 'gainst the brick wall next to the small one-story blue and white painted dry goods store. Chile, he had on a raggedy T-shirt with holes all in it. His pants was barely hanging off of his bony behind and his beard had grown down to his belly button. And the nastiest smell was waftin' up offa him like he'd done wallowed with the pigs and hogs over on Mr. Bacon's hog farm … they lives down the road from the church.

Yes, he was a sight to behold, and when I walked by him on my way to church, I thought to myself … how could somebody turn out like that? Truly, I believe that all he needs to do is go to church and get with us good folk at the church of the Good Lord God and some of the brothers would help him … if he was to start bringin' his old wine-o self to Church.

Anyway, I went on to church 'cause the longer I peeped at that wine-o, the wetter I was gittin'. I just couldn't understand how nobody could let hisself throw away their whole life thataway.

I'm glad I chose to go once I got there, but when church let out I went back down the same way I came. But this time I didn't notice the neighborhood wine-o. "Wonder where he went?" I asked myself. Well, I didn't want to say nothin' to im if I seen him anyhows. I just wanted to compare myself to him, as a Bible-toting woman of God ... and him just a throwin' his life away. My goodness, the life that the Good God Lord done give him ... and he done kicked his blessin' to the curb.

Now, that night, I was sawin' wood ... but good ... when suddenly, my party line done rang me 'woke. I began to shout, "Oh My God ... don't tell me that ... say what ... chile, you have got to be kiddin' me. No! No! No! ... not the Church of the Good Lord God? Not at The Church of The People!

"What happened, Grandmama?"

Chile, somebody ... some low-life such-and-so done broke into the church and stole all of the Holy Wine that we gonna use for the Communion on Sunday. Yes, the very wine that's drunk up to remind us of what the death and resurrection of Jesus Christ really means ... Shanghai'd ... hijacked ... bushwhacked.

So, I got up early Monday morning and ran over to the church to find out what happened, and when I got there, the Sheriff and his deputies and the Pastor, along with the every committee and board member of the Church of the

People was there ... and they was ready to form a posse. All we could think to ask was who could have been so disrespectful to God? Who would lower theyselves to stoop so low as to take from the House of the Lord? After we finished asking each other who could have done such an awful thing, we decided to pray and ask God to help us. We needed God to help us to get over the bad feeling that came over everyone who was part of the Church of the People. All week folks was fumin'!

The next Sunday morning the church was full of people comin' for worship ... and even a bunch of folks who wasn't members of the Church of the Good Lord God was there. I spo'se they came to see how we was doin' after what we'd been through. After the announcements was given out ... and the choir done sang two or three good songs ... everything got real quiet.

Everybody seemed to turn their heads ... all at the same time ... toward the back of the church. Chile, some tall, sharp-looking man had just walked in ... who nobody recognized ... at least at first that is. We didn't recognize who he was 'cause, Chile, ain't nobody, including the Pastor ever dressed that nice in our church!

Anyway, the man's clothes looked like he had walked off of the pages of a fancy men's magazine. You know like Robert Hall or somethin' like that. Let me tell you how this man was laid out lavish. The man had on one of those kinds of rich-lookin', dark, lightweight, wool suit, with gleaming engraved gold cuff links on the sleeves. He had on one of the most glorious looking white-as-snow French collar shirt I'd ever seen …'cept in a man's magazine like I said before. And he had on shoes that look like gator-skin. Chile, they was black and shiny as the sun just breaking on a summer mornin'. He had a nice haircut that had a slight touch of sheen on it … cut close to his head. His beard was short and trimmed real nice. Chile, he did not have one speck or ashy spot on his face or hands. His watch had to be a $50.00 watch 'n fob. Now I couldn't see his feet under those sheer, silky-lookin' black socks he had on, but Chile, that was not the most unique thing about this man. No chile, the spirit that was surrounding him was calm and genuinely lovin'. Truly, we could see that he was not just a well-dressed man … but it was obvious that he was a most blessed man. And Chile, we sure's shootin' wanted to know who he was.

As he walked towards the front of the church he began singing a song that made everybody cry, including the deacons who was sitting on the first pews. The song that he was singing was *I've Been Redeemed*. By this time, Pastor Don'ttakenostuff asked him who he was … and he said, "My name is Child of God! "No!" Pastor Don'ttakenostuff said, "I asked you what is your name? But again the man said, "I told you that my name is Child of God." Becomin' a might peevish, Pastor Don'ttakenostuff asked the man his name one last time, but the man only had the same answer.

He said, "My name is Child of God! However, Sir, most church people have been accustomed to callin' me the neighborhood wine-o. In fact, that's what most of the members of this church done figured me to be for the past 10 years.

"Let me tell you all something", he said, "I came in here last Saturday night and took the Holy Wine from the kitchen cabinet. By this time, our church members and visitors alike began to whisper and say all manner of negative things about the man … me too! 'Specially, once we heard him say that he was the neighborhood wine-o for the last 10 years and that he had stolen the communion wine from the church last Saturday night.

But he stopped them talkin' once he began to tell 'em what happened to him after he got back to the corner store with the stolen wine last Saturday night.

He said, "It was after midnight when I reached the store. I wanted a drink real bad and I knew that the church had real wine for the ceremony you all do once a month. So, I came in through the back door and stole the wine, and when I got to my special place on the side of the country store near the trash heap, I started to put the wine bottle up to my mouth and I heard the voice of the Good Lord God. You see I knew it wasn't one of my wine-o friends cause they couldn't get my attention like that. 'Specially to stop me from taking a sip of wine as bad as I needed it at that moment. Anyway, the voice of the Good Lord God said, 'Son, please stop throwing your life away like you have been for the past 10 years. You see, I understand why you have been letting yourself go. Yes, my son, it all began when your wife and 7 children were killed in a fire at your home, on Christmas day, over in Cabbagegreen County, Alabama. And as soon as you buried them, you left that town and moved here. You did that so that you would not have to think about losing your family. But the memories followed you here. Right, didn't they? "Yes", I said to God.

And then God said to me, "I know that you lost your job of 25 years cause you had a difficult time dealing with people who were blaming you for the fire that killed your whole family. And I know that the doctors diagnosed you as having cancer of the throat. Right?" And I said, "Yes" to the Good God Lord.

And God said, "So, now you're homeless, right? And I said, "Yes", to the Good Lord God. Yet, instead of condemnin' me, He lovingly began to mend my broken and fragile heart, by asking me one very important question.

He asked me if I wanted to become His child. And I said "Why?" And He said, "I gave up my Son for you almost 2000 years ago on the Cross on Calvary's Hill ... and on that Cross He died for your sins ... yesterday, today and tomorrow. So, at that point, I began to cry and I said, "Yes God, I want to have you come into my heart."

So, God did put the love of Jesus Christ, His son, into my heart … and now I am redeemed! I am no longer a wine-o and y'all will never be able to call me a wine-o ever again. You know it still sort of hurts me that none of you ever took the time to talk to me … including you Pastor Donttakenostuff. You are the Pastor of this church, aren't you? Until today, none of you knew who I was. You see, had you walked in my shoes, your hearts would have been different toward me. But that's all right now, 'cause, I am a new person in Jesus Christ and God has healed me of cancer and the pain of losing my family and my need for drinkin'. God has also given me a new beginning, and believe it or not, cause I am now saved, my heart is telling me not to hold what you did to me against you …'cause God is not holding my sins against me. But, you know what you all did to me by ignorin' me and talkin' about me still hurts. Yes, it hurts mighty bad. But my new heart in Christ Jesus says that God will judge your hearts on that matter. Anyway, I am a new creature in the Good Lord God and I want to be baptized as a way to show outwardly, that my internal spiritual condition has changed for all eternity.

The man then turned and asked if there were any visiting preachers in the church, and one stood up and said that his church was located about 20 miles away north of The

Church of The People. The visiting Pastor asked why the man now known to everybody as Child of God, asked that question.

The man said, "The Good Lord God has given me a new life and I don't live too far from there and I want to become an active part of a church near where I now live. And if you don't mind I would like to come to your church as soon as possible to be baptized. So, he got the address to the other Pastors' church and he turned and walked away like a Duke, or an Earl or a King, as he began to sing, "***Walk Around Heaven All Day***".

Children, I have never felt so low in my entire life up to that point. And I fell to my knees and asked God to forgive me of the sin of payin' that man no mind … and a whole lot more. I hope and pray that none of you will ever judge a person by what you see … but that you would go to 'em in the love of Jesus Christ and help 'em.

Don't let folks look at you and say, "There goes that hypocrite Christian! You say you love the Good Lord God … but I'm not so sure. Where's the evidence? And most of all, children, the Lord, Jesus Christ, wants us all to remember and live by **Matthew 25:31-46.** This is where He is separating the real lovers of Jesus Christ from the pretenders and the unbelievers. So, be careful how you treats folks … 'specially if you decide to judge 'em yourself. 'Cause, how we treat others, is as unto Jesus Christ Himself!

THE BAPTISM

… And this water symbolizes baptism that now saves you also—not the removal of dirt from the body, but the pledge of a good conscience toward God. It saves you by the resurrection of Jesus Christ, who has gone into heaven and is at God's right hand—with angels, authorities and powers in submission to him.

1ˢᵗ Peter 3:21-22

The next story Grandmama told us is about the Baptism at the Church of the People. She said that the day started out just wonderful, it seemed. And we asked her what did she mean by, it seems like everything was wonderful?

Well this is what Grandmama told us …

You older young'uns go on out to the garden a pick some dinner vittles while I tell the younger young'uns this little story that still tickles me to this day. It's about a Baptism that we done near 30 years back … well, not we … exactly. I believe I was near about 40 years old at the time and life was great because I was working real hard in the church, just like I am now. On this particular Sunday morning, we had a strange request from a family that wanted all three thirteen year-old male triplets to be baptized … all at the same time. Problem is, we only had one pastor, Levi Rivers … and it mightcoulda been one Pastor too many. He didn't have nobody to help him, 'cause the congregation was small and he thought that he hadta handle everything for his small congregation.

He let us know that he couldn't baptize but one triplet at a time … not one set of triplets … but just one single triplet child at one time. 'Cause, you see, he had a bad back and the triplets was all least six foot tall … even though they was teens. Pastor wadn't but about 5 ft. tall … and that was with shoe lifts inside his shoes.

Anyway, the pastor tried to cut a deal with these children's folks, 'cause he was fearful that he couldn't make their whole request, 'cause of his bein' too small and all. So, when I got wind of what all was going on, I figgered, ya know, that since I done been workin' so hard in the church all these years, that I could help Pastor baptize them children … and keep them parents happy and all.

Really, I didn't see no problem with it 'cause I was a strong woman, especially at that time of my life. Well, children, I went over to the church to see Pastor Rivers because I wanted to tell him that I could help him baptize them children, since he had a problem with baptizing that many children at one time and not having no help.

But children, He told me No ... straight out No ...'cause, he said, no woman is s'posed to help with the real spiritual matters of the church like baptisms and such. He said that it was all right for me to lead the other women in the kitchen cookin' the collard greens, sweet potatoes, macaroni and cheese, spoonbread, fried chicken, slaw, fried catfish, lemon and coconut pies.

But, that a real man of The Good God Lord would never let a woman of the weaker sex help a man baptize ... or do any spiritual thing, 'cause of what Eve done in the book of Genesis. You know she got Adam in trouble eatin' the apple and after that a true man of God shouldn't never allow a woman to be the cause of the devil cursing anything else ... especially a Baptism and all.

Well, Pastor Rivers, went and sat on the first pew and dropped his head to think of a solution, because the family had a lot of money and he figgered them as folk who might-could give a lot of money to the church, so he had to come up with a way to do what they wanted. Children, he sho'nuff didn't want to lose the money they might could give the church.

He said that he would just lay all of the triplets out on the ground near the bank of the lake where we did the baptisms, and he could just pour a coupla buckets of water over 'em and pronounce that they was bein' baptized in the name of the Father, The Son and The Holy Ghost. But, Children, when the childrens' mama, Sister Banks, heard the plan, she said that she would have no part of such a fool thing. She said all through her family line, which went as far back as when the first slaves that came over here from West Africa, her family had been baptized *in* a lake ... not *by* a lake and she wouldn't have it no other way. I heard that the triplets' father, Joseph Banks, agreed with his wife. So when Pastor Rivers heard what they had done decided, he know'd he had a problem, especially with that money situation.

So Pastor Rivers musta got to thinking 'bout the fact that the family had a lot of money and that he would be foolish to let them get away and join up with another church ... and lose out on the blessing's from the Good Lord God.

I could see the dollar signs circlin' 'bout in his thick head, whilst he thought 'bout it. Well, after that, he said. All right, I will baptize the boys my own self, next Sunday morning.

The Banks' was satisfied and told Pastor that they was lookin' forward to it. Then they left the church smiling, thinking 'bout their sons' baptism next Sunday.

In the meantime, I was kinda riled 'bout Pastor Rivers telling me that I was OK in the kitchen, but I couldn't help out with real spiritual things in the church. So, I just went on home and left it to the Good Lord God to pierce Pastor's heart, because I knew in my heart that The Good Lord God always seems to choose the foolish things in this crazy world, to turn the so-called wise folks into addle-minded fools. That means they wadn't all too bright in the brain.

Don't you know that the Good Lord God don't like ugly, because, come Sunday morning, I got to the church house early so's that I could make sure that all the women was there makin' up the Baptism meal ... because that's all we ever was allowed to do ... so far as serious spiritual matters was involved.

Children, I was in the kitchen chopping onions and as I looked out the window, I saw somethin' that would really put tears in yo' eyes.... besides the onions. Pastor Rivers was crossing the dirt road next to the church house, when all of a sudden, a wild hog come a runnin' down the road, and, wouldn't ya know, that hog-wild hog ran right smack into Pastor, knocked all 5 foot of him 'bout 20 foot up in the air, and, even though the ground 'round the lake is soggy, he looked like he landed mighty hard. I heard him screamin' like a loony bird and cursin' the Good Lord God up one side and down the other. Hearin' Pastor talk at God like that put a real hurt on me ... but not as bad a hurt as it put on Pastor Levi Rivers, who musta broke both legs and his good arm ... and his face was all bloody and muddy at the same time. Oh, that was a mess! And don't you know, he broke the very arm that he was gonna need to baptize those

3 triplets later that morning, not to mention the two legs that were broken, that he was gonna need to balance hisself in the water. Some of the Sisters ... the big ones ... gathered Pastor up ... fussin' and cussin' ... and set him down ... out of harms way ... I hope.

Now, some other body else was gonna hav'ta do the baptizin' of the triplets or else the Banks' mightcould end up leaving the Church of the People ... and takin' their long green money with 'em. So, Pastor Rivers asked me ... in between his bouts of cussin' and fussin', if'n I knew any other pastors livin' nearby who mightcould come make the trip to do the dip ... the Baptisin', that is. I told him that I thought making a deep spiritual decision like that was too much for me to do, 'cause I might lead the man of God astray ... like Eve done to Adam ... so I couldn't help him ... 'lest I might do some harm ... and I sho'nuff felt like harmin' him ... but the Good Lord God done already harmed him good 'nuff!

And wouldn't ya know it ... just then ... the whole batch of Banks' children and their kin showed up, ready to have *all* them boys baptized. But, when they saw Pastor Rivers laid out on the side of the road ... all broke down, bruised and bloodied, Sis. Banks turned to him and said, "Well, it looks like you ain't gonna be baptizin' my boys today ... or no time soon ... so, I guess we'll just hav'ta go to another church 'round near these parts, and see if their Pastor can baptize the boys today!

Children, I told y'all that God don't like ugly didn't I? Well, Pastor Rivers gave the high sign and flagged me down to come over to him … so's he could talk at me in private. I went over to where he was still layed out and groanin' on the ground, and I leaned over him and asked him, "What can I do for ya, Pastor …?" He begged me to baptize the boys, so the Banks family wouldn't go someplace else to get them boys baptism'd.

This was the chance I'd been a waiting for all these years at the church. But instead, I just stood and looked right through him for a spell … and then I said, "I believe that you was the one done said I wasn't righteous enough to work for the Good Lord God …'cept in the kitchen, you know, like cooking macaroni and cheese, fried chicken, fried fish, sweet potatoes, pie and such. Ain't that right Pastor Rivers? He just looked kinda sheepish and nodded his head. At least his neck wadn't too broke up to nod. But your Grandmama had a little Word for the Man of God. I told him straight up, "Pastor Rivers, I got some Word fer ya … and you can banks on the fact that it comes straight outta the Good Book of

Joel … chapter 2 v. 28 … and it says,

... It will happen afterward, that I will pour out my Spirit on all flesh; and your sons and your daughters will prophesy....'

And beside that ... whilst Eve was chompin' on that apple, how come Adam was just standin' there and doin' a whole bunch of nothin' 'bout it ... never said a mumblin' word. Did you ever think that maybe the Good Lord God knew'd people just wadn't never gonna be righteous enough to stay in the Garden, so's He set 'em both up and used that serpent Satan to make His point.

Pastor looked at me for a minute or two, screwed his face up right tight and said that he was probably wrong ... and that he would be right pleased to have me do the baptisin' for him, so's Sis. and Bro. Banks mightcould feel good 'bout stayin' at the Church of the People.

Children, don't you know that I rose to the occasion just as sure as pastor got slammed to the ground ... and I was surely an able woman ... not 'cause I was a woman ... and I still am ... but 'cause I did it in the name of the Father, the Son and the Holy Spirit!

Whatever happened to the pastor, Grandmama? Chile, he got better and told me that he learned his lesson and that he was sorry for holding what Eve did in the book of Genesis against all womenfolk in the church. Then he said that he wanted the women's folk in the church to help him with all different matters in church … includin' spiritual matters … for as long as the Good Lord God would have us to do it. And children, wouldn't ya just know it … we found out Sis. and Bro. Banks didn't have no kinda bank in the bank … to speak of. Now, ain't that a hoot to boot!

HOW HE GOT OVER

✦

(The Day The Quartet Singers Came to Town)

Oh, sing unto the Lord a new song; Sing unto the Lord all the earth.

Psalm 96:1

Now children, come 'round here. Did Grandmama ever tell y'all about the annual quartet concerts at my church? Well, every year The Church of the People would scrape together enough money to host one of the popular gospel quartets to come and give a concert. Oh, it was always a very blessed and holy day, but this one year it was even more blessed and special, cause the newest member of the group, *The Christian Crusaders Quartet,* was a young man who grew up around here and we all knew him.

They called him "Brand New". That's the name they gave to any new member. After all, most of the men were in their forties, so they would bring in fresh talent and call 'em "Brand New". They never seemed to have the same "Brand New" singer from year to year, but they would always feature "Brand New" near the end of the show, to whip the audience into a frenzy of holiness and high spirit. I suppose these younger men had more energy and fresher voices compared to these older singers who spent so many years squallin' and hollerin' for God. Children, don't y'all know that I also figure they didn't have to pay "Brand New" as big a piece of the pay. That's probably why each group had a different "Brand New" every year they'd come' round to sing at *our* church. Our church wasn't too big but we would pack the place out whenever the quartet concert would roll 'round. Yes indeed children, we'd have a high ole time in the Lord

Usually the groups would come by after our Sunday Service for a fellowship meal. We loved to get the chance to meet 'em and try to make 'em feel welcome. Then we'd all go home so's they could rehearse, I guess, and set up for the big concert. They'd also set up tables in the lobby so people could buy their latest 45-RPM record, that's the little ones—You know, those little records with the big round holes in the middle. Oh, and the labels be so pretty and every one had a fast song on one side and a slow song, usually an old hymn or preachy tune on the other. I s'pose the fast ones were for the young folk and the hymns were for older folk like me.

They'd also set up tables with fancy Bibles and pretty ladies hats and you could get your picture took with one of the singers for a quarter. Children if only y'all could have seen me, cause I would buy the highest hats and hang 'em to the hilt Believe me, I was the sharpest woman come fifty miles of the Church of the People. Yep! I was one good-looking woman and I ain't bad now. Anyway, since we had the best cooks at The Church of the People they would get a special table to sell the most delicious food—spicy, crispy fried chicken and fluffy soft biscuits and fresh chopped collard greens with jowl and neck bones. Chile they even had sweet potato, cherry, rhubarb and lemon cream pies for sale—cute little ones so's folks could finish—wouldn't hav'ta drag the rest of it home. Believe me chilren they had the best lemonade and cold soda pops anybody could ever get. It was always a beautiful time when the quartets came a-croonin' to sing at our church.

Well, like I said, this one year, "Brand New" was a young man from right 'round here named Silas C. Legum. Silas was a nice young man whose father was a bean farmer just up the next county. His mama died when he was young and I guess he eased the pain of losin' his mama by eating, cause that boy was *BIG!*—tall *and* wide. You know—as big as he was—Silas had a beautiful clear high-silver tenor. It's a good thing his daddy was a bean farmer, 'else that boy probably would have eaten his daddy outta house 'n' home. Yes, Silas loved to eat and he loved his daddy's beans. I'm sure he was lookin' forward to havin' his fill when the *"Crusaders"*, that was their nickname, came through these parts, 'cause they was always travelin' and singin' for the Lord.

Well children, the day for the big concert rolled 'round and we had a beautiful service and our annual fellowship meal. The preacher was filled with the Holy Ghost that mornin'. Now, Essie Mae, you know, little Sadie's Grand-mama—she cooked up a big pot of limas and a big pot of brown sugar baked beans with allot of fatback. She knew that would help "Brand New" feel right at home—and judgin' by the way he tore into them vittles, he was feelin' wonderful. Well, we all went home to rest up for the big concert, while the *"Crusaders"* set up all the music gear and practiced—I guess that's what they did—'cause wadn' nobody was allowed in the church before the concert. Anyway, we didn't wanna see anything before the show 'cause then we wouldn't enjoy the surprise of seeing what kinda suits the singers be wearin', but we knew they'd be "sharp as a tack from here and back".

Well, 8 o'clock rolled 'round and everybody who was anybody was there—and dressed in their best. Let me tell y'all, I had on the finest outfit this side of the county. It was a yellow two-piece suit with rhinestones all the way down from the collar to the hem of the skirt. I had on my finest yellow, patent leather high heels anybody could ever want. And chilren—my hair—my hair was the thing that I just knew everybody would take note on—once they got the privilege to see me. Anyhow, I went a little early to get a good seat in front on the aisle. Y'all see I had to get there early in the front so that I could see who was gonna try to out-dress me and see them fine *"Crusaders"* right close up. I want y'all to know—sometimes being old and cute gets you special privileges.

Well, who am I foolin'?—truth is—mostly being old just gets you old—but sometimes it gets you special favor with folk—and ain't nothin' wrong with that. The Good Lord God wants His children to have favor!

Preacher come up—in his best royal blue, double-breasted, extra-long suit—to open in prayer and call out the group. My, my, my—but didn't he look sharp. I was most proud that he was *my Pastor.* And, when he said, *"… Congregation. Congregation Please put your hands together and give a glorious welcome to … the 'Mighty … Mighty' Christian Crusaders Quartet!! … been servin' in His army near twenty years noe…. the Christian Crusaders Quartet.*

No sooner had Preacher finished when five men came bounding onto the stage—you know, that raised-up area between the right side pulpit and the left side pulpit. They was all clappin'—tight on the backbeat, stomping their feet and sweatin' already. They had on the shiniest lime green double-breasted extra-long suits with matching patent leather shoes and ties—over their sunburst orange dress shirts. Oh, but they was somethin' else!

They lit up the whole room—and lit into the first number—and it was a fast one. Yes, the drums thumpin' a steady rhythm … the guitar was a-twangin' notes like a shimmerin' river run wild … the piano player pumpin' for all he was worth and the bass player hittin' sounds so low it made your ribcage rattle. There was five shiny microphones a five voices blendin' like they was surely angels from heaven.

With five singers, I'm not sure why they call 'em quartets, but they sure sounded sweet. You could hear each voice. The lead second tenor was shoutin' out the words while the bass singer switched between pumpin' rhythms and low down harmony. The baritone and first tenor harmonized so tight, a gnat couldn'ta squozed 'tween 'em—and floatin' over the top of everybody was homeboy, "Brand New"—Silas C.

People was shoutin', clappin, 'and swayin' and some was already bustin' out in their holiness dance. I was getting' kinda happy my own self! Well, the spirit was movin' steady even through the slower songs and everybody was havin' a grand time in the Lord. Then about near the eighth or ninth number, the lead singer asked "Brand New" to come take the lead singers microphone—cause it seem like everybody who done sung lead been usin' that one mike. The older singers was startin' to look a might weary as Silas C., I mean "Brand New" hit a note so high and clear and held it for so long that people started screamin' and fallin' out. Then the band broke into a beat so hard and fast that even the guitar sounded like a drum beat, and the audience started surgin' up near to the front—and Silas C. jumped off the raised area onto the floor with his microphone—and you could feel the floorboards rollin' like the waves in the ocean. Then Silas just started squealin' and squallin' over and over … and over. And when the other men started chantin' in harmony behind him, "Brand New" broke into a holiness dance that musta lasted a good two or three minutes. Getting' happy can take a whole lot outta you, even when the spirit is rollin' high—but when the folks seen a young man the size and girth of Silas C.—hoppin' and struttin'—well, the folks just went hog heaven wild.

Now, when the spirit had eased up just enough and the music had settled down just a touch, Silas C., I mean "Brand New", was ready to get back up on stage and join the rest of the singers, but he was surrounded by all those "happy" people. So, he decided to just climb back up on the stage. He was able to lift his tree trunk of a leg onto the raised-up floor, but, po' thang, he just couldn't get his girth up. Two of the other singers come on down off the stage and grabbed one of his huge arms to pull him up—but he was so drenched in sweat he just slipped right out of their hands. Well, Silas C. kept trying to lift himself up but he just couldn't. I figured he was too tired and too big to do it.

Chilren, being the kind of good Christian woman I am, I knew I had to pitch in and help—and I had a seat right in front of the spot where "Brand New" was trying to climb up. So, I pushed a few folk aside—in a nice Christian kinda way. I went right behind him—bent my knee down a might—and laid my left shoulder right up against his sweaty left buttock—and politely placed my right hand on his right buttock—and prayed the Holy Spirit to give me supernatural strength. Well, Silas C. lifted his big left leg one more again—and now, all four of the other *Crusaders* grabbed holt of his two arm pits and I heard a rumble that let me know for sure that the power of the spirit was movin'—and the whole while the players thumpin' and stompin' and pluckin' and twangin'.

And just then Silas C. cut loose with a fit of wind so mighty, that I was thrown backward. Children, my pretty yellow patent leather shoes slipped right off of my feet and all I could do was pray that the Good Lord God would keep them in a safe place until I finished my Christian duty—liftin' him up—Silas C and Jesus. Well chilren, it turns out, the power of wind musta throwed Silas forward, 'cause, when I caught my breath, there he was—sprawled out on his belly up on the stage—like one of them huge catfish folks catch up by the dam—flippin' and floppin'—trying to git hisself together—like an upright Christian s'posta be. I guess the force throwed the other four singers back on their backs—with their shiny lime green shoes kickin' up in the air.

And the whole time, the band never stopped thumpin' out that rhythm and some of the people got so happy in the spirit, they never noticed—but the *Crusaders* all managed to get back up on their feet—including "Brand New". The song ended on a wave of drums and strums and the band broke into a chorus of one of my favorite gospel songs—a tune that got famous by Clara Ward and the Ward Singers, "*How I Got Over*".

Oh chilren, it was something wonderful! I went back and got my fine yellow shoes and sho'nuff, the Good Lord God had kept 'em safe, 'til I could get holt of 'em. Yes, it was a mighty fine time that day. The day the *Crusaders* came to perform at the Church of the People. And remember this children—with the Good Lord God—every day is a "Brand New" day … thank ya, Jesus!

SISTER SHIRLEY'S GREAT MIRACLE!

I can do all things through Him who gives me strength.

Philippians 4:13

The next story Grandmama told us was about the churches special prayer time. Of course she said that the day started out just wonderful, it seemed. And, of course, we asked her what did she mean by it seemed like everything was wonderful. Well, this is what Grandmama told us.

Chile I was sitting in the back of the church just praying that old sister Shirley Lardner, who everybody calls Bubble-butt, 'cause when she walks it looks like she has a bushel basket behind her and it is shaped like a bubble. Anyway, a lot of people had gotten up to get some special prayer. Some went up to ask the Good Lord God to bless them with a new job. Others went up to ask Him to bless them with a new house. Still I heard some ask for some selfish things, like a new hairdo, a new hat with gloves to match, one man had the nerve to ask the Good Lord God to help him get him a new girlfriend. Chile, if y'all could have seen what he looked like, you would know why he got in the prayer line. Forgive me, Lord, but the man was one of the homeliest men I ever seen.

Anyway, I believe that the Good Lord God had to go to His special workshop to grant this man his prayer request. Do y'all know what I heard one woman pray for? Chile, she had the nerve to ask the Good Lord God to give her some new eyebrows. Now, don't you think that the Good Lord God's got more to do than worry about her getting some new eyebrows?

Let me get back to Sister Shirley Lardner before I forget what I want to say. Chile, it was about twenty people standing in line, and trust me, she was the largest one standing. I overheard two of the brothers who have to catch the people when they get slayed in the spirit discussin' about which one of 'em was gonna catch Sister Shirley Lardner, in case the spirit hits hard. Well, they knew that she would fall 'cause she did it every week. Chile, they was serious about which of them would catch her 'cause, about ten men done gone on dis'bility 'cause o' trying to catch up Sister Shirley Lardner off the floor. Chile, I heard that everyone of those men had to get surgery 'cause they was trying to be obedient to pastor—and the Good Lord God—I s'pose. They surely didn't wanna miss out goin' up yonder to heaven 'cause o' bein' contrary—that means doin' things elseways to the proper ways they's s'posta be done.

After a few minutes listenin' in, I heard Pastor Grady Littles whisper for the two men to come to the front of the church and be prepared to catch Sister Shirley if'n an' when she get up to get prayer. Chile, I could see the look on their faces. They was truly frettin' in thought. I couldn'ta been the onliest one wonderin' what mightcould be runnin' thru those men's heads, whilst they was slowly movin' into position to the front of the church? Well, about fifteen minutes went by and it was time for folks to up and get. By this time, the men stopped and asked the Good Lord God for the some strength that He gave to Samson, you know the man in the bible who killed an animal with the jawbone of a donkey. They prayed real hard for the Good Lord God to give them the strength to be able to obey Him and Pastor Littles. Truly, they didn't wanna disappoint—neither one of them!

I don't rightly know why they always gotsta be callin' on the church elders to do all the serious chores in the church. Mightcould be that some elders is just too old to be holdin' up that much woman. After all, they ain't been callin' 'em elders all these years 'cause they young and hearty. These menfolk be almost old as me!

Anyway, all of a sudden I witnessed somethin' I wouldn'ta believed my own self, if'n I ain't seed it my own self—with my good eye. The muscles in the arms of those men done growed to 'bout a foot 'round in both arms. Chile, I ain't never seen anything like that in all my days. Just as they went to get in the right spot for catchin'—up behind Sister Shirley, there came up a loud sound from the sky and a voice rose up. It musta shouted something only those two chosen men could hear and understand, 'cause it seems like nobody but them was movin'. The Good Lord must have told them that he was well pleased with them 'cause He knew that the situation was too hard for them two to handle—what with catchin' Sis. Shirley and all. Chile, I tell you, it always pays to obey the Word of the Good Lord God in all things. Anyway, Pastor Littles walked up to Sister Shirley and got to whoopin' and wheezin' in prayer over her.

Then, all of a sudden, it seemed like she was shrinking. Chile, it seemed like the woman who everybody had seen weighing about four hundred pounds—on a good Sunday morning, that is ... she just kept on a shrinkin'—right before our very eyes. The brothers stood back and began to praise the Good Lord God for performing a great miracle for them. And Chile, we could hear Sister Shirley crying out to the Good Lord God to help her lose some weight, so's she wouldn't no longer be a burden to the elders of the church—if'n and when she ever felt the pull to yield—to the move of the Holy Spirit—and fall to the floor. I will tell y'all, the Good Lord God is good all the time, and all the time the Good Lord God is good! And you can thank goodness for that!

Well, Sister Shirley went up before the Pastor to have him bless her. I guess the lesson that I learned from the miracle of Sister Shirley Lardner, was that if'n you don't ask the Good Lord God for whatever you want—in faith and in truth—you just won't be blessed the way that you need. I know without a doubt now, that there is nothing too hard for the Good Lord God, 'cause what he done for Sister that day, was truly a miracle!

THE COAT OF TOO MANY COLORS

Deceit is in the heart of them that imagine evil: but to the counselors of peace is joy.

Proverbs 12:20

Children, did I ever tell y'all about the time the young people painted the church? I'll never forget it ... and either will Pastor, 'cause it gave him an idea for a real good title for his Sunday sermon the following week ... and there was some good lessons in the story ... for the young people like y'all

Anyways, it probably happened back in the early 1960's ... I remember 'cause of the music the young'uns was playin' back then. There was this gal named Etta James ... and she took this song right out of the church called, "Something's Got A Hold On Me" and turned it nasty. That old song was about the Holy Spirit working in people's souls ... but when that gal took it, she made it seem like it was about something altogether different ... and not all too savory, if you know what I mean ... and hopefully, children, you don't. Anyway, the teens liked that mess and I used to hear 'em blastin' it outta those little portable radios all the kids carried back then. They'd carry 'em so close to their ears that it's a wonder they heard a car horn honkin' before it near run 'em over. But that's what all the teens had, and when Pastor wasn't around to tell 'em otherwise, they'd be boppin' down the street gyratin' to that kinda mess. They used to call Etta James, "Big Red", cause she was a light skinned gal ... looked like half-white ... and she wore this dyed red-blond wig ... with her big bones ... and her big legs ... and hind parts that seemed to near spread across two counties in her skin-tight mess of a dress.

Anyhow, Pastor had an idea to help those teenagers keep busy, doing something good and positive ... something that would help the *Church of the People* and give them a chance to earn a little money doin' some honest-hard-work. Now some of those kids knew about honest-hard-work 'cause they growed up on farms out from town ... and farm work is hard. It starts at sunup and lasts to sundown and there's nothin' easy about it. Then again, some of the other kids been right spoilt by their parents. They'd do a few simple-easy-chores 'round the house ... and might even get a little pocket money for doin' it each week. On a farm you don't need to get paid, 'cause you get fed real good ... fresh meats ... and fresh vegetables ... and all you can eat. None of this canned junk ... all salted-down with no good flavor ... probably no good vitamins in it neither.

Anyway, Pastor talked the teens into being responsible for paintin' the outside of the church. The children liked the idea ... mostly 'cause of the money, I s'pose ... but it sure enough was better than the plenty-of-nothin' they spent most of their free time doin'. Heck, I've been out here toilin' in the Good-Lord God's vineyard so long ... takin' care of this one and that ... making sure things are done ... and done righteous ... that I forgot what free time felt like. It seems the womenfolk always stayin' busy. Yeah, the men work hard now ... but they always seem to carve out a good chunk of time to play hard too. Maybe that's why us womenfolk are so strong in the church. We too busy to get in a whole lotta trouble. I should have me a little slice of free time now, but I'm sho'nuff busy watchin' after you little hellions. Now one of you go into the kitchen and pour Grandmama a nice tall glass of lemonade so I can finish this story without comin' down with a case of dry-mouth. This mightcould take a while.

Now Pastor asked all the young folks if'n any of 'em wanted to work on paintin' the church, that they should oughta come by on Saturday so's they could plan it out right. He felt like every part of the job should be planned out ahead of time ... and a different somebody should oughta take responsibility for bein' in charge of each part of the job. One to estimate how much paint and supplies to buy … one to see to it that members let 'em borrow the ladders and dropcloths and such … and one keep track of the supplies so's the paint be properly closed up and all the cans accounted for … and he wanted one person to be the supervisor for the whole shebang, so's all the other people in charge had someone they had to answer to … and pastor wanted the kids to take on the responsibility to decide which ones would be responsible for which tasks and who would be the big boss of the whole shebang. That way, if there was a problem, Pastor'd know whose shirttail to yank down about it.

It seemed like a good way to teach these wild young'uns to take on their share of responsibility … kinda prepare them for when they got a little older and responsibility was an everyday-all-the-time thing. Pastor told 'em that it was more important to take their time and do it right … cause if they did a sloppy job and there were places where they had to do it over, that would cut into the money they'd be gettin' to do the job. Pastor was right, too! Like the song says, "99-and-a-half" don't get it when you're workin' on the House of the Good Lord God.

Problem is, young people don't like to wait for nothing … nohow … noway … and Pastor probably knowed this …'cause he was young once … and 'cause he got the Holy Ghost in him to guide him. There's nothin' the Good

Lord God hates worse than folks who got to have whatever whim they want … and got to have it right here … right now. That's like sending an engraved invite to the Devil to start messin' with ya. That demon feeds on impatient People and young folks are naturally ripe for the pluckin'.

Well, if'n it was up to me, I woulda put the kibosh on it whole shebang … but the kids picked Jake Cheatham to be the big boss. Knowin' Jake like I do, it don't surprise me none. That boy can sell ice to Eskimos … just like his daddy, Jacob, Sr. Heck, half the town bought insurance from Jacob and it's hell to pay if the monthly is a day late, but just try to collect on a righteous claim. It'll take forever and then some … but he sure has got the silver tongue when it comes to sellin'. I suppose that's why Pastor has him runnin' that fund-raisin' committee. You can have it. I'd sooner be the one to tell Pastor how best to go spendin' that money, once Jacob done gathered it in. But I didn't have no say in who would be boss of all the teens paintin' the church … and that's a shame.

I got to give it to Jake. He's a natural-born leader. Problem is, the House of the Good Lord God needs a "Supernatural" leader … and Jake wasn't nearly there yet. But I s'pose it ain't rightly fair to expect a young person to be ready to lead that a way.

So Jake, asked Vera Naylor's son Harmon to check the prices on the primer, paint, paint thinner, scrapers, rollers and such. Pastor told 'em how much of each they'd need. Now there was only two hardware stores in town, the one on this side of the tracks and the one on the other side. That wasn't much of a choice now was it?

I suspect Pastor done already priced it out, but he musta thought it was a good lesson for the kids to learn to check it out and add it up for theyselves. They got the prices and added 'em all up, and then they gave the list to Pastor, and his amount was a little more than the amount the kids done come up with. They probably thought they could use Pastor's figure and squeeze a little extra profit out of it. But Pastor's price was really the same as theirs ... they just forgot to add the sales tax. Young folks who never had to pay taxes probably wadn't thinkin' about that, but us grownups know that you can't duck Uncle Sam ... or the great state of South Carolina neither ... when it comes to taxes.

Little Dusty Fields, Harv's youngest, was in charge of gettin' buckets, ladders, dropcloths and such. That was probably a good choice 'cause his daddy and all his uncles was farmers and they had plenty of those kinds of things. Fulton Shedd's boy, Woody, was in charge of keeping track of all the supplies. Fulton has a big empty cabin on his property and he lived right next door to the church ... so that made sense too. After all, the boys couldn't do the paintin' during the week 'cause they had to go to school, do their school work and take care of their little everyday kinda chores before they could tackle a task as big as painting the church. The church building wasn't big as churches go … and I'm glad for that. After all, you want folks to know each other. But it was bigger than most of our houses.

Now, Pastor met with all the boys on Friday evening to go over the Dos and Don'ts of painting. Some of 'em already knew some of it, but Pastor wanted to be sure they was ready to do a real good job. Well, Saturday rolled 'round and the townfolk was surprised to see those young folks up and ready at sunup. It looked like the Pastor was right. This work would keep those teens busy for a while … and out of trouble. He already told 'em they couldn't play no raucous music on their radios 'less it be good gospel music. They didn't. Fulton woulda heard 'em if they did … but they didn't. Pastor had got the word out to all the adults to steer clear of the church so the young'uns wouldn't feel like we was lookin' over their shoulder every few minutes. Pastor really wanted to show them teens that he could trust and respect 'em … in the hopes that it would make 'em proud to be responsible for somethin'. That was a noble notion … but only time would tell if it was a wise one.

The whole town was buzzin' and curious to see how it looked but we didn't wanna cross the Pastor, so we steered clear. The building used to be painted red … not like a barn … but like the blood of Jesus … there to cover you and make you brand new … oh glory! And now those kids was gonna paint it white as snow … just like that "milky white way", after our souls been washed in the blood and walkin' that Straight Street walk for a good while … like your Grandmama! I was startin' to get excited just thinkin' bout it … and I know I wasn't alone. We couldn't wait to see our church all aglow in that great getting' up Sunday morning the next day. I suppose Brother Fulton seen 'em workin' but he must not of told nobody … else word surely woulda got back to me. Ain't much happens 'round here that your Grandmama don't know 'bout.

Well, when sundown came, word is folks started kinda drivin' real slow by the church … like they was on their way to somethin' they had to do … but they was probably just being nosy. Heck, I wished I knew how to drive a car so's I coulda eased on by to check it out, but it was probably too dark to see … and the Good Lord God don't abide folks stickin' their noses in things where they don't rightly belong … but I was surely tempted. I thank the Good Lord God I can't drive no car … so's I wouldn't be tempted that way … and that ole Devil couldn't use me for his devilish purposes … whatever they may have been. I don't know—and I don't wanna know, Thank ya!

Anyway, the evening rolled on and the lights outside the church was turned off at nights anyhow … so there was probably a whole lotta nothin' to see and I just did my little chores pickin' up around the house, got on my knees to pray ... just like I always did ... and lay me down for a nights sleep, the Good Lord God willin' ... and if he still'd be willin' next mornin', I'd get to get up ... clothed and in my right mind ... and head off to go churchin' in a bright shiny white building.

By the way, children, don't let nobody tell you to pray without getting' down on your knees ... or even all the way down flat on your face. That's the only way to present proper to the Good Lord God. We can wash the stains out your pants but you can't wash your own soul clean ... you goota come the throne of grace ... to the mercy seat ... but first you gotta come proper ... in right relation ... let the Good Lord God know right from the get ... that he's the boss ... not us! Some of these so-called Christians ... well, I don't mean to say bad about the Presbyterians and Episcopalians ... but they think that being a standup Christian means never havin' to bend their knee to the Good Lord God ... like they don't really know who's boss ... like they think they be runnin' the show and not the Good Lord God his self. It's simple children. How on earth you gonna touch the hem of His long flowing robe ... and be made whole ... without getting' down. If that hurt somebody's feelings, then oh well ...'cause right is right. It's like the old sayin'; I don't like it and God don't neither!

Well, the next morning … just like I prayed it … I woke … got dressed … and was feelin' just fine and ready for my Sunday in church … in a buildin' with a shiny new covering. I just knew it would be glorious. I planned to get there even a little earlier than usual … well, even if curiosity done kilt the cat … surely Jesus can bring 'em back! I walked the three blocks and I could see the back of the church … it looked pretty much white … but the sky was a little hazy and I wasn't all too happy with the mornin' dew coverin' my shoe. As I was about to turn the corner I started to hear some commotion … and wouldn't you know … the whole church body was gathered outside mumblin' and grumblin' low … and then … as I got a might closer … I started to understand why. The church had a coat of new white paint but you could still see some red showin' through … and the Pastor looked like he was *really* seein' red. He didn't say a word … he just gestered for us all to come in and we had church as usual. But, at the end of the service, he made a special point of thankin' the teens for paintin' the church and asked 'em all to stay after so's he could pay them their due for the work they done. If it was up to me they'da got a whole mess of nothin' and then some. But Pastor ain't like that. He's a quiet, thoughtful kinda man. I woulda tore up some hind parts. I s'pose that's just *another* reason I ain't the Pastor. Now don't get me started!

All the teens stayed after church and Pastor asked everyone else to head on home to pray for his strength and guidance and give it up to the Good Lord God to handle. People was speculatin' on what mighta happened and how ... but it was only speculatin'. Only the Good Lord God and those young heathens knew the real deal ... and Pastor seemed sho'nuff determined to find out for hisself. That Wednesday at Bible Study, he was able to tell us all what really happened, and there was a bunch of good lessons in it, children.

It seems that after everyone was picked to do their part to see that the job got done right, Jake got a notion in his overworkin' little brain that they could make some extra little money by skimpin' on some of the supplies ... and being that he got his connivin' and convincin' ways from his daddy, Jake talked the other boys into goin' along with his plan. Now, if'n Jake had the Holy Ghost workin' on the inside, he mightcoulda stopped hisself from hatchin' his scheme. Put me in mind of the "Little Rascals". I wonder if they still makin' picture shows? They was always schemin' their way into a heap o' mess ... but they was funny ... and real cute. These teens were way too old to be cute anymore.

Turns out Jake convinced those other boys that they could mix some paint thinner into each can of paint ... and since paint thinner cost a whole lot less than paint, they mightcould pocket the difference once they got paid. They saved the store receipt and gave it to Pastor after he gave them the money to buy the paint at the hardware store. Then that evening after it was dark some of 'em went and got half the paint cans out and the next day they took 'em back to old man Sawyer's hardware store, switched 'em for paint thinner and pocketed the difference. If old man Sawyer went to our church they couldn'ta got away with it, but he was one of those stand up Christians ... and white.

Don't ya know, the next Saturday the teens had to put another fresh coat of paint on the church and they wasn't getting' paid for it. They gave Pastor the money they split up and had to work the rest off mowin' the church lawn and rakin' the leaves around the church each Saturday for the next two months ... and they sho'nuff wadn't gonna be playin' any of that mess they liked to hear on the radio whilst they was doin' their chores. Pastor had 'em listinin' to WWAY ... the station that played nothin' but good old-time gospel music.

The very next Sunday, when we all gathered for church, the building looked white as snow ... pure and beautiful. Pastor preached about how sometimes we come to the Good Lord God all wrong from the start. He preached about accepting Jesus into your life at the alter call. He said, "when you truly come to the alter to own up to your mess and accept Jesus Christ as your Lord and Savior in sincere faith ... the spirit that has lived in us since before the beginning of time, takes on a supernatural power that strips off the old paint in our lives and primes us for the promise … but we still gotsta put in the hard work … applyin' the new coat of shiny white paint ourselves. If you come to Him wrong … without sincerity or real faith … He ain't gonna cut the supernatural power of the Holy Spirit a loose in our little lives … and the Holy Spirit Can't make you clean … and once you become a child of the Good Lord God, you are expected to travel on Straight Street and follow the lead of the Holy Ghost".

In other words children, being a right child of God takes effort and work every waking day. He'll meet you wherever you are and clean you up real good for free, but the rest is on you … and believe me … we all got a little bit of devilment in us … and we gotta watch ourselves … elsewise that ole devil mightcould think *he* can run your life … 'stead of Jesus. And if you let him in, that's on you. It may be tight but it's right … and walkin' the walk takes work. You gotta kneel and pray … study the Bible every day … and know fo' sho, that the Good Lord God gots ya … even when things look real bad. After all, he's kept me all these years and he'll do the same for you … Hallelujah Jesus … Glory to God … thank you, Lord!

Well, to finish the story … the People at church was all excited 'cause Pastor was preachin' from the Word and from his true heart and soul … and that's a mighty powerful combination. Some preachers got a true heart for Jesus and don't know diddley 'bout the Word in the Good Book … and some Pastors know the book backwards and forwards … chapter and verse … and ain't got a clue about the Holy Spirit. Pastor got both in bunches. So he called all the teens up again and this time he laid hands on Jake Cheatham and asked the whole church to stand and extend their hands and close their eyes as he began …

"Lord … we come to you right now …

knowing that you and you alone are Lord of all things.
We ask that you touch these boys …
that they might have an understanding in the spirit …
that you alone have bestowed marvelous gifts and talents
upon them …
and that marvelous gifts can become powerful giftings …
when they are applied to your will and purpose.
Please forgive them with your tender mercy and saving
grace …
and bless them, Lord, for the marvelous work they've *finally*
done …
for your beautification of this house of worship …
and we ask all these things in the name of our Lord and
Savior …
the source of ALL salvation, Jesus Christ …
and the children of the Good Lord God say … AMEN …
AMEN … and AMEN!

The whole church was clappin' and praisin' God … and young Jake was flat out on the floor … slayed in the spirit. His daddy, Jacob, Sr., had his hands raised up … tears of joy streamin' down his face. See children, Jake's daddy knew that there's no insurance on earth like the blessed assurance in heaven … hallelujah! All the parents was huggin' their teens and it was a truly glorious day for the Church of the People.

Oh, by the way, the program the ushers handed out that day had the name of Pastors sermon right there in great big letters on the front page …

CHILDREN OF GOD:
YOU MUST *RE-PAINT* …
AND THIN NO MORE!

TURNER ROUNDHILL: HIS WAYS ARE NOT YOUR WAYS ... ANYWAYS!

My thoughts are completely different from yours," says the Lord." And my ways are far beyond anything you could imagine. For just as the heavens are higher than the earth, so are my ways higher than your ways and my thoughts higher than your thoughts.

Isaiah 55:8-9

Children, I wanna tell 'bout one of the young men at the church who really caused a stir with the usher board some years back. His name was Turner Roundhill. Ya see, at the *Church of the People,* we got our own special way of doin' things when it comes to collectin' our tithes and offerings. Do you know what tithes and offerings is? No? Well, the Good Book says that we 'spose ta take a dime outta every dollar we get and give it back to the Good Lord God, and that's called a tithe. Then, all the other kinds of money they collect at church is called offerings. Now, that might be to pay for the big June picnic, or the big August tent revival, or to get Pastor a birthday present or to help some folks who might be in a bad way ... maybe sick in the hospital ... or folks who lost their homes or whatever else come up that needs the help of the church.

Now, just between you and me, I give plenty ... as much as I can anyhows ... but if it be less than a dime on the dollar, the Good Lord God knows, 'cause I tell Him 'bout it ... and He's okay with it 'cause He knows I love Him ... rich or poor ... and you know, Negro folk ain't usually got a whole lot extra to give. But that ain't s'posta be an excuse to be stingy. After all, the Good Lord God loves a cheerful giver, but I ain't gonna take food out any grandbaby's mouths over it.

Well, at church we got our own special way of gathering the money from all the folks at church so's everybody can give and everybody can see everybody givin'. I 'spose it mightcould be a way of shamin' folk into givin' regular, but that's OK 'cause some folks would just be spendin' their little bit extra on some kinda mess or another ... and get theyselves in hot water with the Good Lord God. So, ya see, the church be helpin' folks keep they bidness straight with God. But, like I said, we got a certain way of doin' things and

Turner Roundhill was messin' up the way we always do things … without even knowin' it … and those ushers was mighty peeved over it.

The ushers is those ladies in the white starched outfits with the little white hats and tight white gloves that shows folks to their seats. Now most of the people at the church, like me, don't really need no usher to help 'em to a seat, 'cause most everybody already knows where most everybody else be sittin' every week … the regular folk that is. But whenever a visitor comes in or one of those half-steppers who mosies into church every now and again, the usher ladies hand 'em a program and set 'em on down. Otherwise, one of 'em mightcould sit in my special seat … or one of the Elders seats … or one of the other seats up front saved for the folks collectin' the tithes and offering … and all hell mightcould bust loose right there in church … and the Good Lord God likes His bidness done right … in decency and in order. So, when it comes to seating, the usher ladies give the orders and they do a decent job of it most times … until Turner Roundhill and his family come to town and those ladies started getting' their starched dresses all in a bunch.

Turner's daddy, Roland was a great big man who moved here some years back to work at the bank. Matter of fact, he was the first Negro man ever to work at the bank who wore a shirt and tie. The only other Negro at the bank just be there to sweep up after the bank closed. But big Roland was a somebody in town and his wife, Tessie, had a good job working for the banker's wife, Verdie Mae Blanchard, tendin' to her four little hellions. Tessie was the sweetest thing, but I know those children musta tried every drop of patience she had, 'cause Verdie Mae spoiled 'em rotten. You children won't haveta worry 'bout none of that from me. I couldn't spoil ya if'n I wanted to ... and I don't want to neither.

The usher ladies was already a might testy 'bout Roland, 'cause whenever he got hisself slayed in the Spirit, it took four men to move him outta the way, and we only had three elders, but Turner really sent those usher ladies scramblin'. When it came time for Pastor to call for the baskets to collect the money, the band would play this special little shuffle number and the usher ladies would strut in ... one in each aisle. Then they'd go row to row starting from the back and each person would file out to the big aisle in the middle, with two lines coming down front. The folks sittin' on the left side of the church would put their little money in the basket on the left and then they'd go to the left and file back to their row goin' along the outside aisle up against the wall. At the same time, the folks sittin' on the right side would move row by row to the center wide aisle, come up and give their little money in the basket on the right ... go to the right and march back to their seat up the outside aisle along the right wall. All the while the usher ladies be wavin' folks this way and that to make sure it would be done just right. Pastor would stand there and greet folks and smile ... and he'd really smile when he heard the crinklin' sound and sorta smile when he heard the clinkin' sound. When it worked it was kinda nice to see.

Problem is, Turner would steady be putting his money in the wrong basket ... or come back to his seat up the middle aisle, getting' in other folks way and folks started to chucklin' and callin' him "Wrong Way Roundhill". Turner didn't seem to mind none, but I know his mama and daddy was a might flusterated over it, especially since Turner was a grown young man. Tessie told me he's always been that-away. Now, Turner's a nice and friendly as he could be, but he just couldn't get it straight in his head which way to go and which way to turn. So, it seems the usher ladies got together with the elders and asked the Pastor to hold a special meeting to figure out a way to deal with Turner ... else there might could be a sit down strike by the usher board ... and they never sit down 'cause that's their job ... to stand up through the whole service. Can you imagine that? A strike at the *Church of the People* ... Lord, have mercy!!

I shoulda been invited to that meetin' 'cause I can come up with some pretty good ideas when it comes to getting' 'round obstacles ... and even though I been at the church long as anybody ... and a lot longer than most, I wasn't on the usher board. Maybe that's 'cause I never ushered. I know how to usher, but I got no good reason to wear starched tight dresses and gloves and such ... and I sho nuff ain't standin' up in church all day ... 'ceptin' when the Pastor reads the scripture ... or when the Spirit moves me to jumpin'. Other than usherin' there ain't much the menfolk let us do. I guess that's just the way it be. Anyways, Miss Gabrielle is a good friend o' mine, and she was on the usher board. She can't keep a secret for nothin' neither, so I knew I could get the bird's eye lowdown from her. If'n you got any bidness you don't want gettin' 'round, be quiet when Miss Gabby's nearby ... that is 'less you want all your bidness in the street. Of course, if any of my grands got any business worth keepin' secret, I'm bound to get wind of it, and then some hind parts will surely be throbbin' ... and I mean your'n.

Well, anyway, turns out the ushers wanted Pastor to pull Roland aside and ... in a nice way ... to talk up some of the other churches in town, hopin' that Bro. Roland might take a liking to one of 'em. Nobody had to tell me that Pastor didn't much like that idea. Besides Elder Grubbs, the church money-counter, said that the Roundhill's was good tithers and that a check came in every month from none other than Miss. Verdie Mae Blanchard, the lady whose hellions Tessie been takin' care of ... and that ain't nothin' to sneeze at. Everybody knows that when white folks give ya some money, must be plenty more where that come from. That's what they mean when they talk about "long green". Negroes may have a little somethin' to throw in the pot, but white folks might could have a lot to put in the pot. Everybody agreed ... from Pastor on down ... that we didn't want to do nothin' rash ... and kiss that cash goodbye. The Good Lord God didn't bring us this far to act foolish. Still something had to be done. The folks that snickered in church at "Wrong Way Roundhill" was startin' to hurt the service ... and I know the Holy Spirit wasn't gonna abide no disrespect in His building.

Somebody figured that we might could let the Roundhill's sit in the front row ... and that way they'd be the last ones to get up to put their tithes and offerings in the basket, but the front was saved for the elders and their families and the older folks who was too frail to walk all the way up and around the church every time it came to taking the money. Seems like nobody could come up with a plan to work, so Pastor asked everybody to pray on it and let him think about it for a spell ... and he asked the ushers to hold on just a little longer. So they prayed on it and asked the Good Lord God to send the Holy Spirit on down to help 'em find a way outta no way. After all, that's what the Holy Spirit's 'spose to do ... to guide us on through when we can't see a way clear ...'cause His ways are not our ways ... and I thank the Good Lord God for that ... otherwise we'd be all messed up instead of all blessed up.

Next day I run into Pastor at the butcher shop. I was buyin' me a mess of chicken drums to feed all you little vultures. Pastor was tryin' to act kinda cordial ya know, but Grandmama could read his face ... that he was a might troubled about somethin'. Now, I couldn't let on that I spoke to Miss Gabrielle, else she get caught blabbin' and I'd lose my little grapevine, so I played it cool as a cuke. Then the Holy Spirit gave me a notion to invite Pastor over for some fried chicken with biscuits, sorghum, collard and peach cobbler for the last. I don't mean to crow, but ain't nobody who knows me can walk away from an invite to eat some o' Grandmama's chicken drums ... especially a Pastor. Lord knows preachin' can make a man hungry. So Pastor come over that night after y'all ate me outta house and home. Y'all didn't know I put a half dozen drums in foil just for Pastor. That foil keeps the flavors seepin' into the meat even after it be outta the oven. That gave me a chance to feel him out.

Well, children, by the time he started in to chompin' his fourth leg, Pastor started feelin' a might better and I told him I was worried about him lookin' so blue earlier. He tried to shrug it off but I told him that the Holy Spirit spoke to me and said that I needed to help my Pastor out.

So Pastor gave in and swore me to keep it to myself. It was hard for him to tell me ...'cause I ain't on no committee, ya know ... but it was hard for me too. I had to pretend like I didn't know what was goin' on. You know, children, I shoulda been in the movin' pictures, 'cause Pastor didn't 'spect a thing. After I let him get it all out, he heaved a little sigh. Heck, it was just like burpin' one of you young'uns when you was real little. Just a few gentle strokes and pats and the feelin' starts getting' better near right away. So I let him know that I was feelin' him and that I had an idea that mightcould work all around.

Next Sunday when I went into the church, the ushers were lookin' crisp and struttin' crisp and Pastor was lookin' just fine. Maybe the Holy Spirit was with me ... even though I said that to him jesta get Pastor to let me in on his worry. As a matter of fact, it's probably best to give the Holy Spirit all the credit, anyways, 'cause that what the Good lord God wants us Christians to do. I took my usual seat in the front on the far end and already seated next to my seat was Tessie and Bro. Roland and Turner. Pastor announced that Elder Smalls was being raised up to Deacon. He was the scrawniest of the Elders and had himself a heck of a time when it come to catchin' folks when they fall out after somebody lay hands on 'em or haulin' 'em up after they fall out on their own. Now Deacon Smalls got to sit up behind Pastor and egg him on when he'd get to goin' in his sermon. Deacon Smalls loved to egg on the Pastor and now he got to sit in one of the big chairs back 'o the pulpit. He was beamin'

Meanwhile Roland Roundhill became the new Elder, takin' the spot left by Deacon Smalls, which was good, 'cause the Elders was 'spose ta be an upright church members and not be fallin' out too much, so's he could catch and haul up other folk. Elder Roundhill was just gonna have to keep hisself together, except on special occasions when everybody be fallin' out ... and he was big enough to haul up anybody else who might need haulin' ... and catch any folks who might need catchin'. Then Sis. Weaver, who used to hold one of the money baskets and who always wanted to be an usher lady, was made usher lady in training. That way any usher who got tired of standing all mornin' every Sunday ... or who had to move outta town ... Sis. Would be ready to step in ... and she could step and shuffle and strut. 'cause she was a dance teacher at the Junior High ... has some strong legs.

But the best part was that Turner became the new money basket holder and he got to sit in the front row. That way, he'd be the first one to step up and the last one to sit down and couldn't get in nobody's way when it come time to collect the tithes and offerings. Bro. Gathers ... he's the other basket holder ... he knew that if Turner got up to pick up a basket and went to this side ... that he'd just go on and take a basket and go to the other side. You see children, nobody ever knew it, but I had a little chat with Miss Addams, the white lady who taught 'rithmatic over at the High School, and she was Turner's teacher. Her husband ran the butcher shop. She didn't know why Turner couldn't tell his left from his right to save his soul, but she told me he had a special gift with numbers like nobody she ever seen. Ain't that somethin'!

You know the Good Lord God makes right sure that every one of his childrens has a little something that makes 'em special … something they can use to give right on back to the Good Lord God … and Turner wasn't no different. God's got something special for each of you children too … and each one gonna be a little different … so's there's no need to get jealous of what gift others got. It's different gifts for different givin'. If we had our choice of gifts, everybody be wantin' the same coupla gifts … the ones they think would make life easy for 'em. But if that happened, nothin' would ever be easy and nothin' would ever get done … and done right that is. God's got it all worked out so each gift fits into the others like a huge picture puzzle with a million pieces … and everybody gets to be a little piece … with their special gift. That's just the Good Lord God's way … and His ways ain't our ways … noways … and that's a good thing, "cause we'd just mess it up.

Anyway, Miss Addams was right on the money. Turner was a whiz with numbers. Matter of fact, he could tell you how much was in his basket as soon as the last crinkle or clink rang out ... even Elder Grubbs couldn't do that. He had to go in the back after service and count it up ... dollar by dollar and dime by dime ... and that mightcould take some time. Yeah ... he'd count Turner's basketful too ... but don't ya know, the number Turner'd give him ... that he'd tally up in his head ... was always right on time ... to the dollar and the dime.

I felt good for Turner and for Pastor ... and I was kinda proud of myself too ... even though I gave the Holy Spirit His due for makin' a way and savin' the day. But mostly I felt good for Tessie. She was so proud of her boy and so glad that the snickerin' stopped. I think she musta made Miss Blanchard privy to it too, 'cause the way I hear it, that monthly check from her got a little stronger and a little longer ... green that is.

MANNA FROM SIS. HANNAH

And the Lord was gracious to Hannah; she bore two sons and two daughters.

1st Samuel 2:21

Children, did I ever tell you about Sis. Natalie Hannah, the prayin'est woman ever to come to The Church of the People. She didn't carry no special title … didn't pray just any old time she was asked neither … and didn't much concern herself with what people thought of her. Matter of fact, there wasn't nothin' about her would make you to notice her much at all, but she had the power of the Holy Spirit like no person … man or woman … that I ever laid eyes on. She had the Spirit so strong it scared folks, but she was just as plain and calm as could be … most of the time.

Now Pastor didn't call on Sis. Hannah every time there was a call for prayin', cause nobody ever knew just what mightcould come out of her once she let the Holy Spirit take over her body ... and it was her whole body that moved in the Spirit. But Pastor knew that whenever it was time to really birth some baby Christians, wasn't nobody could deliver the goods like old Sis. Natalie Hannah. If I could I'd give her a special title: Midwife of Mercy.

You see, Sis. Hannah had a special gift, and like pastor always say, "the Good Lord God gives every child of God a gift that they be extra good at ... and some folk get a bunch of gifts ... but unless we use them gifts to build up the Kingdom of the Good Lord God, it don't mean diddley. Now that's my word, not Pastor's, but you get what I mean don't ya?

Look at Sam Cooke. He had a beautiful gift to sing like a bird and write righteous gospels that tell the stories in the Bible in ways that regular folk could understand. But he took that extra special gift that the Good Lord God give him and took it away from God to chase down dollars and dollies ... and look what happened. He got himself shot dead by some strange woman in a sleazy motel room, and when they found him he was naked as the day he was born. What a shame and a waste of the gifts that the Good Lord God done gave him and him alone. And what's worse, the best gospel singers in the country are all going the same way now ... chasin' dollars and dollies instead of the Kingdom. God help 'em!

Now, on this one particular Sunday morning Sister Hannah was sitting quietly in her favorite spot near the back of the church. It was communion Sunday when all the children of the Good Lord God took the bread and the wine, and this particular Sunday, we had a very special visitor ... the overseer, Bishop William B. Wright. Pastor would call him Will outside church, but in church we knew him as Bishop Wright, and he only came once or twice a year, so Pastor probably wanted the Bishop to see how we was bringin' new folks into the church. Well, after he warned everyone that if they take the bread or wine in an unworthy manner ... that means if they ain't confessed and taken Jesus into their sorry lives to save 'em, there would be hell to pay.

I guess since the Bishop was comin', Pastor brought out the big shiny silver wine pourin' pitcher ... and it was sure shined up nice. And Pastor and Bishop was both dressed up in their best black robes with beautiful bright trim. They almost looked like kings or somethin'. Then, after we *right* Christians took communion, Pastor asked some of the folks that didn't take communion if they was right and ready to accept Jesus Christ as their personal Lord and Savior. I s'pose he figured if'n they wadn't right enough to take the communion, that they mightcould be ripe for the harvest ... and about six People stepped forward. Now understand this good, children, you gotta really be honest about taking Jesus in your life. It ain't no fad or fashion … ain't no fakin' 'til ya make it … it's all about faith … and when the Holy Spirit finally moves folk to step forward in faith, he enters 'em with a new power they ain't never had and it's the bestest feelin' that ever was. But lotsa folks just step up 'cause somebody done pushed 'em or shamed 'em into it … and the Spirit ain't buyin' it. That's why ya see the same old sorry People comin' up and fallin' off and comin' up and fallin' off. But if they'd come right and true, then they'll know fo' sho', the Good Lord God is real and the Holy Spirit'll be there to walk with 'em and talk with 'em. But the Spirit don't abide no bunk!

I guess Pastor wanted to let Bishop Wright see how Sis. Hannah birthed those babies. Maybe Pastor seen her often enough that he forgot how scared he was the first time Sis. cut loose the Spirit, but he sho' nuff didn't know what to make of it then. That's kinda the first reaction of most men folk to Sis. Natalie Hannah's special gifts. It scares 'em. Well, Sis. walked up from the back of the church dressed kinda plain, especially compared to the robes Pastor and Bishop had on and the fine suits the Elders and Deacons was wearin'. Then she did somethin' I don't think nobody expected. She invited Bishop Wright down front and asked him to lay hands on the folk while she prayed. Bishop looked kinda glad to be doin' somethin' 'cause through the service he just kinda sat in the big chair behind the pulpit lookin' important and noddin' his head to show he was pleased. Pleasin' the Bishop was a good thing for the church and he was pleased to help.

Well, children, Sis. started in to prayin' hard and fast and before you know it, she was doubled over like she had a stomachache. She started speakin' in tongues and groanin' like a woman in labor ... and shakin' and twitchin' and sweatin'. The Deacons and Elders started getting' up and movin' back away from her like they was scared, and Bishop had a look on his face like a deer caught in the headlights of a steady movin' car. The folks who came up to accept Jesus started into shakin' and movin' round and shoutin' out loud, and then Sis. Hannah started in to talkin' in a loud moanin' voice like it was the Good Lord God hisself talkin' right through her ... and you could hear her say just as plain as day, "you claim to be a man of the cloth but you do not do my will and you have three children by women who are not your wife. Repent and beg for forgiveness or the Lord your God will strike you where you stand!"

Like I said, ain't nobody know what mightcould come out of the mouth of Sis. Natalie Hannah once the power of the Holy Spirit takes over. One of the Elders and two of the Deacons fell down on their knees crying out to God to forgive 'em and the Bishop ... well his eyes bugged out and he started into shakin' and couldn't near stop. He started in to sweatin' like a runaway slave. I mean the water was just pourin' off him. He tugged at his robe and unbuttoned his collar like he was chokin'. I guess in a way he probably was a runaway slave ... a slave to sin and runnin' from hisself ... that is if Sis. Hannah hit it right when she spoke her prophecy. It was a sight all right! Those new Christians was bouncin' and shoutin' just as happy as could be, while the Bishop just kept takin' hankies from the Elders and Deacons and soakin' 'em through. Lord, have mercy!

Well, Children, seems the Bishop Will B. Wright got hisself moved to a different district. Pastor said before the service ended that afternoon that he didn't abide no gossip and that we was to pray for the men of the church, that they yield not to temptation. Sis. Natalie Hannah just walked on back to her pew as calm as could be. I'm not sure she really knew what happened that day and she probably ain't too much concerned about it. She just knew that ..."when the Lord gets ready ... you got to move."

As it turned out, four of those folks that come forward that day been good faithful members of The Church of the People. Sis. Natalie moved on a few years back ... probably birthin' baby Christians for some other church ... with no worry and no title. Fact is, you don't have to be a Deacon

… to be a beacon … and shine the beautiful light of the Good Lord God in front of you … wherever and whenever you make your walk. That's what we all s'posta be doin' everyday, it's just that that was Sis. Natalie Hannah's special gift.

One of these old days when the menfolk let go of their stiff-neck ways and let women be preachers too, Sis. Hannah will be leadin' lotsa more lost souls to the throne of grace for the sake of the kingdom. Seems like men just don't much wanna be 'round when babies are bein' born. Come to think of it, when gals go into labor and the doctor ain't around, men call the midwife to take care of business while they make themselves scarce. Or if they go to the hospital with their wives, they're shooed out in short order and just stay in a waitin' room chompin' on nasty old cigars and tellin' bawdy jokes. But havin' babies ain't no joke. Ain't much different with birthin' Christians. In all my years, I ain't never seen any man … and only a few special ladies, could pray the way Sis. prayed. That shouldn't surprise nobody, I guess. After all, men don't know nothin' 'bout birthin' no babies! It ain't always sweet and oftimes its downright messy and hurts like I don't know what … but when you see the faces of those new creations, ain't no question it was all a wonderful blessin' for us who receives 'em and for the Good Lord God who keeps 'em. Thank you Jesus!

BROTHER LESTER'S BATTLE

However, each of you also must love his wife as he loves himself, and the wife must respect her husband.

Ephesians 5:33

Children I am going to share with you something that I never want you to forget.

Always remember that there are things that we bring into our life that God has not destined for us.

I wanna tell y'all something 'bout folks that's married. Yes, people who done chose to get married to somebody that they think is their *soul mate* … someone they believe is the best person for them for the rest of their life. That's what brother Lester Boulware believed when he married sister Tori. Children it took me a while before I realized that brother Lester was living in a fantasy world when it come to love. I remember the day when he brought that woman Tori to the church and introduced her to the congregation.

I knew right then that something wadn't quite right 'bout her.

She seemed to have airs … like as if somebody done owed her somethin'. You know somethin' like always giving her compliments and things like that. Believe you me, she did not look worth a nothin', but she walked 'round like she was God's gift to the world. In fact, her attitude made me wanna have nothin' to do with her. That includes going up to the alter for prayer and holding her hands. That's what the Pastor wanted us to do. He felt like if we held each other's hands, that the Holy Spirit would get into every body and he wouldn't have to spend so much of his time praying the devil out of the folk.

One day, children, I seen something that made me wanna cry for brother Lester. On a Thursday morn, while I was cleaning the church kitchen, I happened to hear a man's voice a ways off from where I was standing. The man's voice seemed to be crackin' like he was crying. I felt like I was supposed to go to see what was going on 'cause the Pastor wasn't there. The only People at the church that day was me and the man's voice I was hearing. So, I slowly walked toward where's the voice and it was getting louder and louder. I could hear a heap o' hurt in that voice. As I got closer I could see that the cryin' man was brother Lester. He was on the wooden floor on his knees crying out to God about his wife. I heard him say these words:

"Dear God, I am really hurtin' inside ... my heart is achin' ... my life seems empty, 'cause that wife you done gave me is trying to kill me. Yes, the wife that you gave me God. The pain I'm feelin' been going on since the second month after we done got married. It started with her tellin' me to give her *all* the little money ... and she'd start throwin' things at me if'n I didn't give her everything she wanted. And that included telling her everyday that she was the most beautiful woman in the county. Fact is, Lord, I seen her stand in the mirror saying things to her own self 'til she started believin' she was the beautifulest woman 'round these parts.

God there's been times when I woke up in the morning, only to find her standin' up over my bed, threatenin' to kill me if'n I didn't buy her some somethin or other she wanted.

Yes, God, the woman that you gave me ... the woman that you done fashioned for me for the rest of my life. I didn't ask you for her, you just gave her to me.

Children when I heard brother Lester talk to the Good Lord God that way, I was ready to hit the floor and start prayin' for him my own self, 'cause he was about to bring the wrath of God on his own head. Who ever heard somebody talk that way to the Good Lord God? Children, what brother Lester was doing was sho' nuff askin' for a heap o' trouble from above.

Anyway, I just stood there with my heart just a flutterin' 'cause; I couldn't believe what I was hearing. I didn't want him to know that I was standing near him, elsewise he might stop talking to God and leave. But he just kept right on a prayin'.

> "My heart is hurtin' inside 'cause of that woman you gave me. She scares me all day and night. I can't hardly have no peace. God, I can't even pray when she's 'round. If only I could fly away like a dove, I would. But my children, what would they do? God, if I could just get away to really pray. Sometimes God, I want to stay here in the church hidden away from everybody 'cause I am so miserable. You know God, that woman that you gave me!
> You know God, if this was my enemy or somebody like that, I could deal with it. But it's my wife … the woman you gave me … who hurts me so bad. She even lies to me about everything. God I thought that she was gonna be special and loving, but it seems like the devil is in her sho-nuff. I can't even hide from her. What am I gonna do?
>
> Last week I had so many bruises on me that I had to wear a long sleeve shirt to bible study. I couldn't let the brothers see that I was so beat up. I thought my wife, the woman that you gave me, would be a sweet companion, a close friend and lover. You know God, some-

body that I enjoy sweet fellowship with when we come into the church to worship you. It just ain't that way for me Lord. I don't know what happened God. How did this happen when I believed that the woman I married was somebody you wanted me to have?

Children, then I heard a still soft voice in a distance say something to brother Lester. The voice said this, "My son, I did not give that woman to you to marry. She is like a Jezebel, a wayward woman who worships idols and I wanted to tell you to avoid her but you never asked me if you should marry her. I don't want you to keep saying that I gave her to you anymore, 'cause, if I had given her to you, you would not be in this situation. I would have given you a woman of virtue ... a woman who would first honor and glorify me ... a woman who would honor you at home and in public ... a woman who would be of a good report ... giving to others and proclaiming my name to everybody she meets, 'cause I am a merciful and loving God."

"My son, I am saddened that you waited until the problem got so big that you are ready to give up. Here is what I want you to do. I want you to repent for not seeking my face before deciding to marry. I want you to pray for your wife 'cause she is in bondage to the enemy. Pray for her deliverance and I will bring her unto myself. My son, I want you and your family to have an abundant life through me, not through your own will. Know that I am in control and I will move the devourer from your home. You will have a peaceful life, a peaceful marriage and your children will grow up honoring me."

Children, as I stood there, I was feeling that there was hope for brother Lester, if'n only he did what God told him to do. You see, children, when we go on our own, makin' big decisions without talking to God first, then we get ourselves in a heap o' trouble with the Good Lord God. I want y'all to promise me that you will always pray to the Good Lord God before you just jump off and do sometin' big ... like pickin' a mate to marry. That'll save ya a whole heap o' hurt in your life. Trust me, children, I had to learn the hard way ... a time or two in my life, just like brother Lester. You see, there is a way that seems right to folks, but in the end pushes God away. That is what the bible says children. The Good Lord God don't wont his children to do what they think is right. The Good Lord God wants us to do what we know is right 'cause, we are living the way the bible tells us to live.

So, after a few minute was gone, I started to walk back to the kitchen 'cause, and I didn't want brother Les to know that I heard his talk with the Good Lord God. After all, what we say to our God is between us and Him.

I made sure that I pray'd for brother Les and his family for a long time after that.

A SOUL AS WHITE AS
THE DRIVEN SLUSH

Then Peter replied, "I see very clearly that God doesn't show partiality."

Acts 10:34

Children, it's time for me to tell you another important story about somebody who used to worship with us at the Church of the People. But first, I want to ask y'all something. Has anybody ever looked you dead in the eye and called you a name that let you know ... loud and clear ... who they thinks you is and ain't in this crazy world we live in. Whatever it is, Grandmama's heard 'em all ... and heard 'em all my life. There's always gonna be demons trying to tell you who's better and who's worser than them ... what folks can and can't do ... and why you shouldn't be somethin' or do somethin'. Know it for what it is ... the work of Satan ... and rebuke those demons in the name of JESUS. And remember ... always use His name when you rebuke a demon, 'cause the Good Book tells us plain that there is power in the name of Jesus … so long as the one that's callin' it is a real true child of the Good Lord God.

Now you don't just want to blurt it out any ole time … in any ole place. Make sure you're prayed up good first and be sure to praise Him up and down, 'cause the power to bind a demon ain't in you or even me … it's in the Lord. Besides, there's some folk that if you say somethin' straight out at the time you feel it, your heart may not be right and you mightcould get strung up … just like Jesus Hisself … but God told Jesus to let hisself get strung up to save our sorry behinds … and no one's tellin' you to do something foolish. That won't prove nothin' 'cept what we already know … that some folks is just plain evil.

I want you to know that no matter what nobody says, the Good Lord God loves his children … and that it's gonna be a rainbow in heaven. Now, here in this crazy world, color means something … and to some folks color means everything … and I'm not just talkin' 'bout white folks. They no different than nobody else … there's good white and evil white … and there's good colored and evil colored … and I've seen plenty of both … and both make my heart ache for the mercy of the Good Lord God … and folks that have evil ideas on the color of folks skin gonna need all the mercy they can get when they try to signify before the judgment …'cause the Good Lord God don't have time for that mess. Matter of fact, the Bible says Jesus had hair like lamb's wool … just like us … and everybody in that part the world had darkish skin. Either you gonna be blessed up or messed up … and if'n you leave this world messed up … you gonna end up in hell … fried extra crispy … and that's no lie!

Now children you need to know that some coloreds got some crazy notions about skin color too … and when I look at all my baby grands … I can see all types of colors … and ain't none more beautiful to me that another … and God feels just the same ole way as me. I've heard 'em all … High yalla … redbone … mocha … coffee'n cream … chocolate … chestnut … smokey … shady … black … blue black … quadroon … octoroon … albino … freckled red. And colored folks go through all kinds of twists and turns trying to look lighter than they is …'cause they thinks it makes 'em somethin' more than they is. Now, I can't say as that I blame folks for it …'specially them that don't know the Good Lord God for theyselves … and white folks treated darker folks extra bad over the years … but that ain't no good reason for colored folks to believe that mess … or act on it …'specially in church. But, it seems that some of the church folks is the worstest ones when it come to judgin' folks by the color of they skin. Fact is, if'n your heart ain't right ... you can't see the light ... skinwise or elsewise.

Now, children, there was a young lady that used to go to church with us name of Blanche Dumont. She had moved here from N'awlins, to be the head of the county schools ... the ones for colored folks, that is ... and she had a good education ... not like me ... and a big-time job ... and her skin was the highest yalla I ever seen. She coulda passed ... for white that is. Even the way she talked sounded just so ... not like the most of us. Her hair was dark with a gentle natural wave to it ... what folks call "good hair" ... not thick and curly like mines. She was one of them Creoles, who got blood mixed with French folk ... and in N'awlins that meant a whole lot. To me, and the Good Lord God, it didn't mean diddley ... but as a Christian woman, I was s'posta abide her ways as a member of the Church of the People ... and that's what I meant to do.

There was some folk who didn't like her just 'cause she mightcould pass for white ... and then there was others, like me, who didn't much like the way she acted. Seems like she'd put on this face like she had sour pickle juice on her upper lip whenever she was around folks she didn't feel right about ... kinda put her nose up and wrinkly. Some of the parents at the schools said that she had her teachers to treat the darker skin children different … like they was more suited to handiwork than schoolin' work … and maybe they was … but it just didn't smell right to me. There's a bunch of different reasons that some folks might think their stuff don't stink … but the Holy Spirit let me get a good strong whiff of Sis. Blanche for my own self … and her stink stunk … just like anybody else who wasn't all the way right.

Well, about a year after she came here, she got married to a man name of Reginald Lightfoot. He musta been part Indian, 'cause he was almost as light colored as she was … and mighty good lookin' if I might say so … and I do … and everybody liked Reginald 'cause he was just plain good people. He worked for the railroad … had a good job in the office there … and it was plain to see that he loved Sis. Blanche … even if no one I knowed could figger why. Let's just say, children, that love has its own way of movin' folks this way or that … and so long as they was happy in their marriage, it ain't none of my bidness … and evidently they was …'cause less than a year after they got hitched up, Sis. Blanche started looking like a lady with child. It looked like a boy child too …'cause she was carryin' real low, like the old wive's tales, and she seemed to spend alotta time runnin' to the toilet. See, babies …'specially when they carry low … sit right on a women's parts that make you feel like you gotta go. It's good practice for later on 'cause a boy child can keep ya sho'nuff rippin' and runnin'!

Now, when Sis. Blanche and Bro. Reggie ... well Blanche didn't much like nobody callin' him anything but Reginald, but he didn't seem to carry airs about it. When they got married, you never seen so much white in your life. Everything was white as snow. I bet the store in town didn't have any more Clorox on the shelf, 'cause all of it got used. It really was beautiful ... but even the food was whitish ... no collard ... no yams ... no ham and such. Folks called it gentile food. I call it white folks food ... and it was mighty bland ... but I'm not gonna dwell on that 'cause the Good Lord God did feed us and I don't need a plateful to be grateful for it. The music they had was kinda bland too. They hired a gentleman they knew to play the organ ... and he could play okay ... it's just that all he played was old slow hymns from the hymnal and I was like to fall asleep. I probably wasn't the only one, but the newlyweds seemed happy and I s'pose that's what matters most on their big day.

Anyway, we was plannin' to throw a baby shower for Sis. Blanche. I stocked up on Clorox and sho'nuff, she wanted everything white as snow ... again ... and she wanted Sis. Bessie to make her something called "finger sandwiches". I didn't much like the sound of that, but I couldn't quite put my finger on the reason why. Turns out they was sandwiches with just a little bitty somethin' between two pieces of white bread, then they cut off the crust and cut the little things in half. No wonder Sis. Blanche was so slim. Needless to say, we didn't eat too much ... but the crows had a feast on all that crust that got cut away. You know, they say that the crust of the bread has most of the vitamins and minerals for your health. Maybe that's why Sis. Blanche looked so peekish all the time. Those bitty little sandwiches didn't last but five minutes ... and some of them big heifers was ready to grumble, but we kept our manners right. After she opened the gifts folks just sorta said their fast goodbyes and rushed on home to eat ... some real food.

As the time rolled on, Sis. Blanche just kept getting' bigger and bigger, until she got to about 2 weeks from the time the baby was due and it seems like she stopped comin' to church. Now I Can't hardly blame her, what with the baby pressin' her bladder and havin' all that extra weight on her little "finger sandwich" frame. But the child like to up and disappeared. Nobody'd seen hide nor hair of Blanche or Reginald ... and we was a might curious ...'specially after givin' her the baby shower and all them cute little things for the baby ... and they like to fell off the face of the earth, so far as the Church of the People was concerned. No thank you cards … no nothin'. Even Pastor was in the dark about Sis. Blanche's whereabouts, so he asked us all to pray and pray hard for Blanche and Reginald and the baby … and we did.

We called the school board and they said she was on leave. I don't know what that means but it sounds nice. I ain't never been on leave and I don't know nobody else who has neither, but it seems that when she gets better her job will be waitin' for her. I ain't never heard of such a thing. Where I come from, if you a no show … that job's a no go!

We heard a rumor that she had been in the hospital in the next county over, but it wasn't nothin' more than a rumor. I s'pose Blanche had some serious problem with the child that she didn't want nobody to know about. Rumors was flyin' and a whole lotta s'posin' was going on. Maybe she had a stillbirth … when the baby be born dead … or a child with some horrible crippled-up child … or simple or deaf or something. After a while the rumors stopped and we sorta forgot 'bout Blanche Dumont Lightfoot and kinda moved on. You know, if you're a child of the Good Lord God … life goes on … within you … and without you … and life without Blanche and Reginald just sorta moved on.

Then one day about a year later word come down the vine that Blanche had moved back to N'awlins. Seems Sis. Heald gots a cousin who worked as an orderly at the hospital in the next county ... and she heard tell from her cousin that Sis. Blanche had a fine healthy baby boy, but that she was so wore out from the long labor that she just didn't want to be bothered with the boy and that she stayed in the hospital even after the boy went home with his daddy. I can't 'magine what would make a mother do such a thing ... but that was the word we was gettin'. I took it with a grain of salt ... that means I wasn't for sure that I believed that story 'cause it smelled a might fishy ... but if'n it was true, it was something more than bein' wore out from a hard labor. Women been havin' babies since Adam and Eve ... and ignoring a newborn baby just ain't no ways natural for a mama ... even one as stuck up as Sis. Blanche. But that was the bidness bein' told on the vine.

I prayed to the Good Lord God that that baby boy ... if he *was* born ... if he *was* livin' ... be healthy ... with all his fingers and toes and two parents to give him love. That's about all I could pray for. There's enough poor babies out here that nobody wants and never should have been burdened with livin' in this crazy world.

Like I said, after a while, people moved on and other folks came and went at the Church of the People and other juicy gossip was swirlin' round and everybody just forgot about the Lightfoots. Then one day ... must have been almost a year later … we was in the middle of our praise and worship service and the house of the Good Lord God was rockin' righteous to the gospel, when the door opened and in come none other than Sis. Blanche, carryin' a bundle all wrapped up in swaddlin' cloth and took a seat in the back of the church and just kinda sat quietly rockin' back in forth. She looked okay. Matter of fact, she looked like she put on a little weight and had a little color in her face that made her look right healthy compared to last time we all saw her. About five minutes later Reginald came in with an old man I'd never seen before. The man was short and bent over a little bit … like folks get when the arthuritis takes 'em over … and he was blue black … dark as the ace of spades. He didn't have too many teeth left and his Brogan shoes and Stetson hat looked older than me … and that's sayin' somethin'!

Once people started to notice that the Lightfoots was back there, eyes started in to starin' and whispers started in to flyin' and Pastor looked a might perturbed that folks wasn't payin' attention to the Father's bidness like they s'posed to be. So when it come time for him to get up to preach, he made a point of welcoming the Lightfoot family. I s'pose he figured he'd best get the curious bidness outta the way, so's the people could focus in on the sermon and stop peepin' and such about the folks in the back row. There would be time for idle chatter and catchin' up after service ... but this was the Holy Spirit's time to open up our hearts, minds, bodies and souls to the word that Pastor was about to put down. He preached loud, long and strong, so's nobody was likely to let their minds wander to other stuff going on in the buildin'. He preached about how the Good Lord God used "... the foolish things of this world to confound the wise ..." and that's why He said that "... the last shall be first and the first, last ..." It was a good word and preached with power and feelin'

All through the service the baby wrapped up in Sis. Blanche's arms didn't make nary a peep, but no sooner had the Pastor finished the Benediction, than that baby child started in to hollerin' like a siren on a fire engine. I guess some of the other little babies in church musta took that as their cue to start in whinin' and wailin', 'cause before you know it, the whole building sounded like a Holy Roller baby roundup.

One by one ... little by little ... the mamas was able to quiet down the young'uns, but Blanche's child just kept on squawkin'. Least we know'd his lungs was okay. I walked up to Blanche and looked at the child all wrapped up in those bedclothes and said, "honey, loosen them blankets and let the child breathe a might. As soon as she unwrapped him he stopped squawkin' and started in to cooin' and gurglin' and wigglin' and gigglin' … just as happy as a pig in slop. I reached my arms out to hold him and Sis. Blanche slowly handed him over to me, but you could see she wasn't all too comfortable about it. But she know'd … just like everybody in town know'd … your Grandmama has a way with little ones.

Well when I looked at him I could barely believe my eyes. I didn't know if he'd be born wrong like the gossip said, but seems like he had everything the Good Lord God meant for a child to have. The one thing I noticed though was that Reginald Lightfoot, Jr. was just as black as the ace of spades and was the spittin' image of the stooped-over old man sittin' next to Reginald, Sr.… but he was for sure a happy baby and I prayed that his parents would raise him up right in love … to be a child of the Good Lord God … who loves his neighbor like he loves the Lord. That's all the prayer any of us really need. The rest of it is just silly stuff to take our attention away from simple wrong and right. As it turns out the old man was Sis. Blanche's grandaddy … and it wasn't until that baby was born that she even wanted to get to know the man who fathered her own father. Children, sometimes people can be so stubborn when it comes to making a big thing outta stuff that don't mean diddley … like the color of our skin … when we forget to lean on Him … the Good Lord God … as our only true covering in this crazy world we live in. Children, there are always gonna be fools that look at you and see nothin' but a nigger ... but make God your cover ... and the light of the Lord will always shine through your darkest days. And from that time on I believe Sis. Blanche learned to love her granddaddy, her baby boy and everybody else the Good Lord God made to serve Him.

THE MAN OF GOD IS SO CRAZY ...

✦

(We May Have to Have Him Committee'd)

Woe unto you, scribes and Pharisees, hypocrites! for ye are like unto whited sepulchres, which indeed appear beautiful outward, but are within full of dead men's bones, and of all uncleanness.

Matthew 23:27

Children, remember this and remember it good. Pastors is people too ... and just like all people, there be good ones and bad ones and they all fall short of the glory of the Good Lord God. It says in the Good Book that Jesus was no respecter of men, but there is one man I'll never forget ... the most messed up Pastor there ever was in all my days at the Church of the People and in all my knowin'. His name was Rev. Dr. Noble Braggs, Jr. Pastor Braggs was put on us after Pastor Sheppard passed, and Bishop Wise told us that this new man was coming to the Church of the People from doin' missionary work in the West Indies … I think that's near China or somethin' … and if'n we liked him, he mightcould be our regular Pastor. Po' thang didn't last six months … and for once it wasn't our crazy ways that chased him off … it was his own doin' that was his own undoin'.

Now he was mighty impressive to look at. Tall, dark and good lookin' and he dressed himself in only the best finery … even if the Mrs. and his children looked a might shabby. And he was educated and talked kinda dicty and highfalutin … said the folks in the West Indies called him Prophet and Apostle and such. Well, maybe that's right and maybe it ain't … but I don't believe the Holy Spirit much likes it when he gives folks the gift of prophetizin', and they want to hang it around they neck like the shingle in front of the doctor's office. After all, you can't go to school for prophet papers. The Holy Spirit gives lotsa folks the gift of the prophets. Even I seen stuff before it happens and speaks in tongue sometimes, but I got 'nuff fear of the Good Lord God not to lay that name on my own self. That might give the Holy Spirit the notion that I don't need Him no mo' … and then He might hold back His power when I really need

Him. No, I'll leave all them titles to someone else and keep the Holy Spirit close by to me.

Well, the very first things outta Dr. Braggs mouth was a list of all the things he was gonna do in the church and all the things he wasn't gonna do … and mostly it was all the things we was s'pose to be doin' for him and his. He said he don't visit sick folks … don't do house calls for prayer … don't do no cleanin' up of nothin' … don't let other folks in *his* pulpit nor teachin' *his* Bible study … don't let nobody take the collection to the bank but him … and don't want no folks in his church that look drunk, shabby, lowdown or po'. He thinks we forgot that part in the Bible where Jesus told pastors to feed His sheeps. Dr. Braggs believed the sheeps oughta be feedin' him … all the time. Now, some folks in the church bought it hook, line and sinker, but yo' Grandmama wasn't lookin' to abide no Kingfish in the Church of the People … and I weren't the only one neither. But we stayed mum and showed respect for the man … for the position … for the time bein'.

So Dr. Braggs goes into a long list of all things he 'spects from us. He said we gonna pay tithes and then some … so's he can put his kids in college someday. We was s'posta pick up his house note … heatin' bill … car note … food bill … and so on. The only thing he forgot to ask us to do was to fold his toilet tissue for 'im when he had to go do his bidness in the bathroom. I was too through! Then he goes over the list of things the church was gonna be doin' ... other than preachin', prayin', and studyin' the Word. We was gonna have Pastor 'Preciation Month ... Anniversary Week ... Advent Week ... Deacon 'Preciation Sunday ... Elder 'Preciation Sunday ... Usher "Preciation Sunday ... Armor-Bearer 'Preciation Sunday ... Food Committee 'Preciation Sunday ... and even "Preciation Sunday for all the folks that be plannin' all the other 'Preciation Sundays. I can tell ya for sho', I didn't much "preciate any of that mess. Wasn't none of it about the Good Lord God!

Now with all this stuff goin' on every week, Dr. Braggs decided he had to start formin' a whole bunch of committees for everything ... all of 'em answerin' only to him ... and he wasn't never satisfied with the way folks was plannin' and doin' stuff ... ever. Lord have mercy. We was all workin' full time jobs or takin' care of our own families ... I was goin' crazy tryin' to keep my grands in line ... chasing crumb-snatchers ... rug-rats ... carpet-crawlers. Then I gotta do the cookin' ... cleanin' ... plantin' and pickin' veggies out the garden ... getting' the older grands to check up on the younger grands home studies ... and all my other chores. So Dr. Braggs called me into his office one day to ask me to head up the Axle-ry 'Preciation Committee ... to plan the 'Preciation Dinner for the main 'Preciation Committee. He didn't know it yet, but the answer would be, NO!

He had a big frilly Diploma in a fancy wide wood frame with gold paint on it, and even the writing was fancy where it said "Doctor of Divinity". It was from some place called Trinity Divinity Bible University in Nassau, Bahamas ... wherever that is? He also had a big picture of hisself in another fancy frame, wearin' a fine suit and holding a big stick that looked like somethin' you mightcould see Moses hisself totin', and on each side of him was these big strong-lookin' young men in black suits, black shoes and thin ties ... one holdin' a beautiful long purple robe with gold trim and the other holdin' a beautiful gold crown with shiny jewels all over it. It was somethin'! He told me he done heard that I was a pillar of the church for a very long time and that I deserved to have a title worth somethin' ... just for bein' me and for takin' care of the Axle-ry 'Preciation Committee. Seems everybody in the church was so committee'd-up, there wasn't no one left but Grandmama. Well, I'm plenty busy bein' 'bout my Father's bidness, that I just politely said no thank you, got up and 'scused myself out.

You see children, people loves to have they titles ...'specially Negroes ... since we been stomped on so bad by white folks for so long ... but titles don't mean much to the Good Lord God ... After all ... He's the Good Lord God and ain't no title nobody could get to top that. So I just be's happy with the little titles I already got. I got my title in this crazy world ... Grandmama to all my Baby Grands ... and my heavenly title, child of the Good Lord God ... and that's just alright with me. But, Negroes love they titles and I think the new Pastor knowed it and used it to get folks to do what he want 'em to do. See, a man may be a janitor or even a pullman porter, and that's a pretty good job, but on Sunday they get to dress up in their Sunday finest and be called Deacon Suchandso or Elder Whoyoube ... and folks feel like they need that little bit of extra somethin' to make 'em feel good about theyselves in this crazy world. Child of the Good Lord God be good enough for me ... and good enough for a place next to Jesus on the throne in heaven ... and ain't nothin' better'n that. You can keep your other titles ... don't make me no nevermind.

All this stuff was goin' on ... people gettin' committee'-up to the ceiling ... titles bein' throwed around to and fro for anybody who was fallin' for Dr. Braggs' notions, and folks was shellin' out cash to "The Man of God" like he was Pharaoh. Meanwhile we ain't heard him preach yet ... and that's the puddin' that the proof be layin' in. Can he put out the Word so's it hits ya in the heart and spirit ... and if'n he can do that, I mightcould put up with all the other stuff. But, if he can't run it down righteous, don't no piece of paper in a frame on the wall mean diddley to me. I was hopin' he'd do good with the Holy Word, but, Lord forgive me, there was a part of me that didn't think he had it in 'im … I mean the Holy Spirit. And without it … Dr. Braggs ain't nothin' but an educated fool … just like folks out there in that crazy world. I wanted to know if he was *washed* in it … and I'd give 'im the benefit of the doubt … but not the benefit of the drought.

Well, Sunday rolled 'round and I gotta admit, folks was dressed up nice and the building was lookin' clean as a whistle … smellin' nice too! I wasn't gonna be left out nei-ther. I paid Sis. Wiggins a dollar extra to whip me up a nice beehive hairdo and I was lookin' sharp as a tack. The onliest ones that wasn't lookin' sharp was Dr. Braggs' wife and kids, who looked a might scruffy again and poor ole Sam Swiggs, who got booted at the door by the two young men Pastor put out there to welcome folk. They played football for the high school team. Sam likes to drink a bit and his clothes look a might wrinkled, but we always let 'im in. After all, you never know when the Spirit mightcould move 'im to get hisself saved for real.

Now, the praise and worship was fine. Folks was in good voice and wasn't no white visitors clappin' on the wrong beat ... throwin' everybody off. Things was goin' along just fine. Then, when it came to collectin' time, Pastor told everybody that he didn't wanna hear no clinkety-clankin' ... only foldin' money and checks ... and he called up Sis. Counce to hold up the basket while he prayed over the collectins. He musta thunk that the higher ya hold the basket, the more money would show up come countin' time. Sis. Counce was the new Chairlady of the Collectin' Committee. She worked as cashier down at the Piggley Wiggley, so's she was good at handlin' money. Well, I mean to tell ya, Pastor broke out into prayin' and he prayed and prayed ... musta lasted ten minutes and he was treatin' the money in the basket like it was God Hisself. Poor Sis. Counce started to drop her arms ... I guess they was getting' a might weary of holdin' that basket up. Well, without missin' a beat, Pastor shouted, "Hold that basket up!" and Sis. looked like she seed a ghost ... her eyes bugged out and she held the basket up as high as her stubby little arms could and when Pastor finally finished prayin' for increase, everybody said, AMEN ... Sis. Counce said her AMEN 'specially loud. Then she turned the money over to Bro. Banks, the new Chairman of the Countin' Committee. He worked in the countin' office at the sausage factory.

Then one of the new Armor-Bearers brung out that same fine purple robe with the gold trim ... like in the picture on the wall in his office … and hung it carefully 'round Pastors shoulders … careful not to muss up his 3-piece suit … and the other Armor-Bearer brung out the wood stick I seen in the picture and water in a big, fancy metal mug with a linen hanky hung over it. Then, Dr. Braggs prayed and called out the title for his first sermon at the Church of the People. It was called, "Showin' Proper Respect for The Man of God in the House of God … and everything he done in that sermon come right outta the Old Testament … Jesus wasn't nowhere to be found in it. Now, of all the things I ever heard any Pastor say over the years … that title … The Man of God … always rubs me wrong … like there wasn't room in the whole round world for more than one Godly man … like they was the 'lectric company and the onliest place to go to get your power. He wasn't the only one I ever heard usin' that title, but it fit his selfish ways just right. No fear of God in the man … 'til it makes ya wonder if he really believes there is a Good Lord God … or he just thinks he be getting' over on folks, so's he don't really gotta work for his upkeep. I knowed plenty preachers held down regular jobs to help make ends meet … but I couldn't imagine Dr. Braggs doin' nothin' but bossin' other folks 'round.

I'm sorry to say children, as long as there's been a church and folks in it that don't know God for theyselves, there's gonna be wolves in sheeps wool … pimpin' the people from the pulpit. Ain't nothin' new under the sun ... and Grand-mama been around long enough to see a good piece of all of it ... every kinda Pastor there is ... some good ... some bad ... and some so wrong that the demons of hell be plannin' to ride right on in here on those preacher's backs. That's why it's up to each one of us to learn the Word ... to under-stand for our own selves ... so's we can smell the stink when there's a mess in the midst. And you need to stay prayed up every day, so the Holy Spirit will be there for ya when you need to know in your sanctified soul, just what's right and just what ain't.

I once heard a real educated man tell it like this ... and it made a whole lotta good sense to me. See, Negro folks come from parts of this world where its hot all day and night ... all year 'round ... and its been that way for as long as Negroes been on the earth ... long before white folks ever showed up and before slavery. So if a man killed hisself a nice hog, that hog would sho'nuff spoil in the heat before he could use all the meat. So folks from hot weather places on the earth formed tribes. That way they could share everything ... nothin' would go to waste and they might-could have a better chance to all make it through another day together. Now some of the white folks lived in places where they could grow food or kill meat and freeze it to use later. They didn't need to have tribes ... they needed to protect their stuff and keep other hungry folks away … so's their stuff could last longer for them. Even though we all got the iceman comin' to bring ice for our icebox today, white folks still seem to love their stuff more than they love people … and Negroes seem to put all their heart in other people and don't do as good a job takin' care of their stuff. Folks are funny that way.

Well, once Negroes got tribed-up, folks might have times when they didn't want to share or might think someone done 'em wrong, so they started pickin' chiefs and elders and formin' councils and committees … just like in church … to keep people from killin' each other and to help share what they had as best they could … for everybody in the tribe. The trouble started when certain kinds of men wanted to bc the chief, but maybe they wasn't the best one for the job … just the biggest or meanest or strongest … but not always the wisest. So, when folks get to start runnin' the show but they don't much care 'bout nobody but they-selves, the whole tribe gonna suffer and only the chief gonna do well. That's what it seemed like with Dr. Braggs at the Church of the People. He done gave folks fancy titles to make 'em feel more important than they needed be, and then he used them to get what he wanted for hisself alone. Lord have mercy on his soul. And that's why some white folks, if'n you asked 'em if they could save their Grandmama's life, but they'd haveta give up all their money, they'd likely as not, spend a quarter and buy granny a real nice goodbye card...."cause their stuff meant more to 'em than they kinfolk. Oh, I'm just kiddin' ... sorta.

After a while, folks at the church started goin' broke and getting' sick and tired of bein' bossed 'round by a bully. I figured there must be some of 'em started thinkin' like me ... that this man had to go. Well, after a few months, folks started murmurin' 'bout this and that and Dr. Braggs would just start changin' people on the different committees and puttin' new folks in old places with new titles ... but the game was the same and when stuff starts getting' really old, the stink of it just don't seem to wanna go away ... and the smell was catchin' up with Dr. Braggs. It was just a matter of time 'fore the stuff that was stinkin' would start hittin' the fan and splatter all over everybody hangin' round.

One Sunday after the sermon, Pastor called up folks for prayer and called Bro. Banks to get the tithe book and bring it up to the front. Five people lined up for prayer, one by one, and Dr. Braggs looked up their tithes before he'd pray for 'em. The good tithers got long prayers, just like the prayers he did over the money every week, but when he came to the sharecropper, Bro. Sowell, and he looked at the tithe book, Pastor shook his head and frowned. Then he put his wood stick on Bro. Sowell's forehead, just like he always did when he prayed for folks, but all he said was:

Hal-a-ba-shonda ... ha-sheeka-ma-shy ... that's all you get, so move on by!

Folks was not happy.... not happy at all! You ain't s'posta ration prayer like it's a gasoline shortage or somethin' ...'specially when we had a drought over the summer and Bro. Sowell's crops died in the field. No wonder his tithin' wasn't strong. And folks didn't much like how Pastor spoke in tongues neither. Seems like every time he wanted folks to think he was movin' in the spirit, he be saying the same little nonsense sounds ... every time ... like he learned himself a nursery rhyme ... but instead of sayin' fe-fi-fo-fum ... he'd always say ... Hal-a ba-shonda ... ha-sheeka-ma-shy! He might be sellin' somethin' but I ain't buyin'! And, thank the Good Lord God, other folks didn't seem to want to buy his line of jive no more neither. Thank you, Holy Spirit. Oh, and by the by, if'n he hadda prayed for me ... touched my nice new beehive hairdo with that nasty wood stick, he'da felt my sting ... but good!

Well, the final straw came when he told the Pastor 'Preciation Month Committee to go out and get a great big banner to put up outside the church for the occasion. When the committee asked Bro. Banks for some money to get a proper poster drawed up, Bro. Banks said Pastor told him that anything that committee ... or any committee had to do, the folks on the committee would haveta come outta they own pocket for it. So Sis. Regina went to the sign painter in town, got a price and found out what size sign she could get for the money she had. Well, as it turns out, "The Reverend Dr. Noble T. Braggs, Jr., Pastor", would not quite fit on the sign. Pastor was not happy about it and made his feelings knowed to Sis. Regina ... and even though he was in his office ... with the door closed tight ... everybody who was left on the Pastor 'Preciation Month Committee heard the shoutin' loud and clear. Sis. didn't budge a bit neither, and told Pastor if'n he wanted the bigger sign he could pay the rest his own self ... and that's that! Sis. told me later that Pastor decided to take off the word "Reverend" cause there was no way that sign was goin' up ... in his name ... and everybody in town wasn't gonna know that he was a Dr. with a fancy diploma in a fancy frame.

That next Sunday, the first week of Pastor 'Preciation Month, Dr. Braggs was just startin' in to a long drawed-out prayer over the offering, when the door opened and a county sherriff's deputy come in. The deputy waited quietly for Dr. Braggs to finish up prayin'. Dr. Braggs saw him standing there and invited the Sheriff to come join the folks and that he was sorry that the good deputy had missed his opportunity to put a little something in the offering plate, but Sis. Price took the basket right on over to the white deputy Sheriff and held in front of him ... almost darin' 'im to drop somethin' in. The deputy fished a dollar out of his pocket while everyone watched in silence. I'm sho 'nuff glad he didn't come in during praise and worship and mess things up clappin' off the beat.

Anyway, the Pastor thanked the Sheriff and invited the man to have a seat near the front. Folks had to jam they-selves together, 'cause all the Chairpeoples of all the committees sat up front and there was so many committees there was hardly any room for the Sheriff and his pistol and his baton and all. Then Pastor turned 'round and signaled his Armor-Bearers to bring up his robe and wood stick.

Just as the man handed the wood stick to the chieftain ... I mean Pastor ... the deputy jumped out of his seat, pulled out his pistol, pointed it right at Dr. Braggs and called out:

Noble T. Braggs ... you are under arrest.
Drop your weapon, get on your knees and put your
hands behind your head.

That was the first and last time we ever saw Reverend Dr. Noble T. Braggs, Jr. on his knees … and it was about time. Everybody was struck dumb and just sat there for the longest time … even after they cuffed 'im and hauled 'im off to jail. I got a tinge of hurt in me for his wife and kids, but when I looked over at 'em they seemed relaxed for the first time in all the time they'd been comin' to the Church of the People. Pastor wouldn't let nary a one of 'em make so much as a peep … ever … and I think the Good Lord God done set those captives free that day. I went over to her to see how she was doin' and to invite her and the young'uns to lunch at my house.

It put me in mind of that picture show, "The Wizard of Oz". You know, when Dorothy spilt that water on the wicked witch … tryin' to put out the fire on the scarecrows arm, and the witch started meltin', I thought for sure all those monkeys and soldier guards who was doin' that witch's bidness would kill Dorothy, the pup and the whole bunch of 'em. Well, they didn't. See, they was glad the bad witch was dead and they didn't have to do her will and mind to her mess no more. Maybe Dorothy didn't mean to do it, but she set the captives free too.

As it turns out, it was all over the papers. Rev. Noble T. Braggs, left his last church 'cause the folks was fed up with his crazy ways and the Bishop must have sent him to us 'cause our Pastor died so sudden, he figured we could try Pastor Braggs, and Pastor Braggs could get another chance after messin' up at his last church. Well, it weren't that simple. See, the folks at the other church thought some of they moneys was missin' and they called in the Sheriff to check it out. Come to find out Pastor Braggs stole $320 dollars, sent it to Trinity Divinity Bible University in Nassua, Bahamas … wherever that is … to buy him a fake piece of paper to put in that fancy frame on the wall. He went to the West Indies to do his missionaryin' jesta get outta Dodge 'fore folks found out about him, and when nobody said nothin', he came on back home looking for another church to milk dry. Sherriff says men of the cloth do that mess … buy a fake piece of parchment sometimes so's they can charge churches more money if'n they come to preach there, 'cause they be Dr. Suchandso … instead of just a regular Pastor. Problem was most don't get caught 'cause they ain't fool enough to steal the money from they own church, to foot the bill on the fake papers.

When the Bishop got wind of it, he was mighty humbled 'bout it … felt bad that he done pushed that man on the Church of the People like that. Well the next week the Bishop hisself preached the sermon and title was, "If you love me, you will feed my sheep". He did a fine job with it too. Then after service, everybody from every committee got together to pick one last committee to help pick a new Pastor. Bishop promised that they wouldn't send just any ole warm body (or cold-blooded one) with the title Pastor after his name. Since I was the onliest member of the Church of the People in good standing ... and not all committee'd-up already, they chosed me to be Chairlady of the Selectin' Committee. I told 'em was glad to do it and I picked Sis. Price and Bro. Sowell to help me. That don't rightly make up much of a committee ... in fact, it was a kinda itty bitty

Committee. But, a month later we got ourselves a new pastor ... the same pastor in charge of the church today ... and he's a good honest man and a good humble shepherd who takes care of all of us right nice. Thank you, Jesus!

GRANDMAMA …
SEIZE THE LIGHT!!

… So if the Son sets you free, you will indeed be free."

John 8:36

Now children, I done told you 'bout every story 'bout everybody ever went to the Church of the People as long as I been there … from 1905 to 1965 … and this crazy ole world is a-changin' plenty 'nuff … but Grandmama gonna hold to the Good Lord God's unchangin' hand … just like always. Some of you young'uns mightcould feel like I'm too old-fashion' to know nothin', but when Jesus left us … after raisin' up from the dead … he left the Holy Ghost to tend to us day to day … to help us along the way … and that same Holy Ghost walks and talks with me near every darn day. If it wadn't for the Holy Ghost, the words in the Good Book would just look like a bunch of nonsense scribbled on the pages. But even with my little bit o' schoolin', I see that

Holy Story … and the Lessons it be teachin' … just as plain as day. Thank you Lord!

Now you children run on 'long home, 'cause Grandmama needs to have a little talk with God … and I need to do it all by myself … in my quiet place. Remember now, I told you lotsa times, can't nobody run your Christian race but you and God, 'cause there bound to come a time when you need help that only God can be givin' … and Grandmama … and Pastor … and nobody be around to pray … or to show the way. It be you and God all alone. So you better sho' nuff know Him for your own self … how to come to Him right and talk to Him true … else this crazy ole world surely will be the death of you … and everybody that means anything to you. All these stories I done told may seem kinda funny sometimes … and they is … but that's only 'cause the lessons I be tryin' to teach y'all is so serious that it mightcould scare you. So, I put a little funny bone in 'em so's they go down a might easier. It's kinda like the honey I put in the castor oil.

That demon Satan ain't big like God … and he ain't got God's power … but you best believe that if'n you give that devil an inch, he'll fashion a cinch to fit just right 'round your scrawny little necks. You'd best believe that and act like you know … like you know Him … and that means studyin' His word in the Good Book. Stay close to the Holy Ghost, 'cause the Holy Ghost is a person … and He got fee-

lins ... just like you and me, and if'n we don't do right in
our walk, He'll get His feelins hurt and leave us high and
dry for a spell ... to fend for our own selves ... 'til we get
our stuff back right, that is.

I hate to tell it ... but seems like folks just ain't gettin'
saved no more ... I mean really saved. Maybe that's 'cause
the Holy Spirit done moved on outta the church. Yeah,
folks come forward when the alter call comes, but more
often than not, somebody done pushed 'em ... or twisted
they arm ... or made 'em feel shamed if'n they don't. If the
Holy Ghost is workin' on you, you'll *sho'nuff* step up to
confess Jesus is Lord and died and rose up again ...'cause
when the Lord gets ready ... you gotta move. But if'n the
Holy Ghost done got up and gone for a bit, ain't nobody
getting' saved nohow, 'cause it ain't about givin' your heart
to God ... it's about God grabbin' it ... in spite of you or
what you think you be doin.

Then, after folks get pushed up to the alter, the countin'
committee can come in and count a new soul bein' saved
and report it to the church section, so's it can go in a news-
letter ... like a bunch o' door-to-door vacuum salesmens in
a sales contest ... tryin' to keep count of who sold how
much. Trouble is, those kinda folks either fall off the wagon
in no time flat, or just play church ... like the folks in the
movies go playin' a role. If you really get saved, everybody

'round ya gonna know it … just by the change in ya from what you was.

There's plenty of half-steppin' heifers … one-day a week prayers … fence-sittin' sinners … Bible-totin' bet-hedgers … stand-up Christian fools … pimps in the pulpit … and just plain ole evil demons out here. Folks be waitin' 'til the last second to get theyselves saved … so's they don't miss out on none of the fun they thinks they's havin' … and they don't even know that the Good Lord God can take 'em out … fast as a pig can slurp slop. Folks just ain't scared of God no more.

I ain't scared of nothin' and nobody out here, but I know better than to be messin' with my blessin', by treatin' God just any ole way. I don't surrender to no man or woman … white or black … but I surrender to God … every day … on my knees … and I pray … that he gonna let me get up offa my knees for one more day … so's I can praise His name … stake my claim … stay in line … and work my vine. Jesus is the onliest King in all history that don't *just* wanna make you His subject. No children, He wants you … all of us right Christians … to inherit the throne and wear the Crown Victorious.

You know I love y'all, but I need my 'lone time … just me and Him … and I'll see y'all a little later … to go on to

Bible study. Now go on outside and play so's I can have a little talk with Jesus ...

Father in heaven ... I praise your holy name ... Forgive me for my sins ... the ones I know about and jes' too hard-headed to halt ... and the ones I don't even know I'm doin'. I know you're comin' back ... so have your way with me, Lord ... right here on this earth ...'til it be my time to move on up a little higher ... and I can live forever with you ... AMEN!

Now Lord ... there's so many things I come to understand 'cause your Son, Jesus died for me ... and 'cause Jesus sent you, oh Holy Spirit ... to light my way from day to day. THANK YOU LORD! But Lord, I gotta know how things in your church done got so crazy ... just like this crazy world done took over the church ... not just Church of the People ... but seems like the Body be wheezin' hard for a breath of You ... and just Caint seem to find the way to draw You in ... all we can seem to do is breathe out ... all that mess we got inside us ... but Caint draw in much of nothin'. I pray ... right here today, Lord, that you will lay your healin' hand on your Temple and set the folk free ... like me.

I got a bunch of questions, Lord and I hope you ain't sore about 'em ... after all ... you woke me this mornin' ... clothed and in my righteous mind ... so's I might so well give my mind a little exercise and ask you 'bout a few things that's been troublin' my spirit for some time now ... 'bout the church and church folk ... 'specially the ones who seems to always be leadin' folks.

Seems like the church today ain't much different than when those Pharisees in the Old Testament didn't want Jesus to set folks free from the rules and rulers in the Jewish temple ... and they didn't want to believe that Jesus was the Messiah, 'cause it might mess up their little games, power plays, and such. I'm sorry, Lord, but so many of them just ain't right ... so please tell me ...

- Why is it so many preachers shout righteous in the pulpit on Sunday and flirt with the girls on Monday, 'specially them gals that go to their own church and trust 'em with their private troubles? Folks have troubles and need help and all these so-call *Men o' God* can think to do is help theyselves ... to every sweet slice of pie stoppin' by.

Revelation 22:11. He which is filthy, [is] filthy still!"

I John 2:15a: "Love not the world, neither the things the are in the world ...

- Why is it so many of 'em drinkin' and druggin' on the sly? Don't they believe their own words when they preach 'bout fearin' God when we ain't walkin' right.

For such men are false apostles, deceitful workmen, masquerading as apostles of Christ. And no wonder, for Satan himself masquerades as an angel of light. It

is not surprising, then, if his servants masquerade as servants of righteousness. 2nd Corinthians 11:13-15

- Why does tithin' mean so much nowadays? I thought them Old Testament sacraments got nailed to the cross with Jesus. Used to be preachers worked for their bread ... like the rest of us. Even Paul, the greatest church-starter ever, made tents for his livin' ... didn't expect church folks to support him for every dime ... all the time. If'n ya Got Jesus, you won't need to cling on these self-serve Saints. And when folk step up for healin' prayer, some Pastors won't help em' 'les they tithes be paid up full. Ain't they s'posta serve ... like Jesus ... not be served. **For the priesthood being changed, there is made of necessity a change also of the law. Hebrew 7:12 When He said, "A new covenant," He has made the first obsolete. But whatever is becoming obsolete and growing old is ready to disappear. Hebrews 8:13**

- Why do so many services seem more and more alike, no matter what church you go to? It's like that new hamburger place, MacDonald's. It be the exact same in every town. I worship Jesus, not McJesus with cheese ... thank ya PLEASE! Father, maybe we need the fire, your fire from above? **2ndCorinthians 3:6, "The letter killeth; the spirit gives life."**

- Why do some Pastors know so much 'bout talkin' but know nothin' bout bein' still and waitin' on You God? Some of 'em seems to be in love with the sound of their own voice ...'til so's the Holy Spirit can't get a word through ... noways ... He might maybe don't wanna be bothered trying for a spell ...'til we learn to shut up and be still. **[I pray that] the eyes of your heart may be enlightened, so that you will know what is the hope of His calling, what are the riches of the glory of His inheritance in the saints. Ephesians 1:18**

- How come folks are runnin' 'round from church to church callin' theyselves Prophet Thisandthat? Seems to me, whenever the Good Book talked 'bout prophets, didn't nobody much like 'em or want to hear what they had to say ... and it wadn't 'til way later ... after their visions done come true ... that they got tagged with them titles. I think Profit mightcould be the real reason these penny-ante fortune tellers wanna claim that title for theyselves.

  Matthew 24:11 And many false prophets shall rise, and shall deceive many.

- Why does every preacher gotta have a bigger buildin' than the next? In the early church, leaders raised up other folks to lead ... and start new churches ... so no churches got so big that leaders might start to think they had a corner on Christians?

And he said, This will I do: I will pull down my barns, and build greater; and there will I bestow all my fruits and my goods.

And I will say to my soul, a soul, thou hast much goods laid up for many years; take thine ease, eat, drink, and be merry.

But God said unto him, Thou fool, this night thy a soul shall be required of thee: then whose shall those things be, which thou hast provided? Luke 12:18-20

- The way I remember readin' it in the Good Book, the New Covenant Church wadn't s'posta have stacks upon stacks of church leaders with high and mighty titles, trying to tell Christian folk when to fast and how to pray … like the Holy Ghost only be talkin' to them. I can talk to you, my God, for my own self. And ain't You sent Jesus here, so's we wouldn't need no priest to save us no more?

For I say, through the grace given unto me, to every man that is among you, not to think of himself more highly than he ought to think; but to think soberly, according as God hath dealt to every man the measure of faith. Romans 12:3

- Why do leaders be addin' new titles to they names all the time …'til you gotta take three breathes just tryin' to get 'em all in … and if'n you be forgettin' one of those little titles, they can get mighty uppity 'bout it? Lord, I thought the Holy Ghost is spose to teach us what you want us to know. Includin, the preacher folk … Now I can see someone gets a diploma for schoolin' alright, but ain't no diploma for prophets, apostles and evangelists. Most of them be self-appointed … and noways anointed. **The very credentials these people are waving around as something special, I'm tearing up and throwing out with the trash—along with everything else I used to take credit for. And why? Because of Christ. Yes, all the things I once thought were so important are gone from my life. Compared to the high privilege of knowing Christ Jesus as my Master, firsthand, everything I once thought I had going for me is insignificant—dog dung. I've dumped it all in the trash so that I could embrace Christ and be embraced by him. I didn't want some petty, inferior brand of righteousness that comes from keeping a list of rules when I could get the robust kind that comes from trusting Christ—God's righteousness. I gave up all that inferior stuff so I could know Christ personally, experience his resurrection power, be a partner in his suffering, and go all the way with him to death itself.**

If there was any way to get in on the resurrection from the dead, I wanted to do it. Philippians 3:7-11

- Why can't Negro folks and white folks ... folks who claim they's prayin' to the same Jesus ... be churchin' together? Now you know that just ain't right ... even if we **think** their service be boring ... and they think ours be too loud ... ain't no time in the whole week, when I see and greet less white folks, than on Sunday mornin'. Sometimes I think white folks is so darn scared of Negroes folks 'cause they knows in their hearts ... that if'n they had to go endure all the mess they done put us Negroes through ... that they mightcould just shoot up the whole place ... and everybody in it! Lord, only you can heal this mess.**There is neither Jew nor Greek, there is neither slave nor free man, there is neither male nor female; for you are all one in Christ Jesus. Galatians 3:28**

- Why do our Negro preachers ... well some of 'em ... gotta act like they the chief of the tribe in some kinda Tarzan movie ... with the thrones and the fancy robes and staffs and Armor-Bearers treatin' em like Pharaoh. PLEASE, PLEASE, PLEASE ... ain't Jesus good enough for 'em? No ... they gotta clown ... like James Brown.... **Also a dispute arose among them as to which of them was considered to be greatest. Jesus said to them, "The kings of the Gentiles lord it over them; and**

those who exercise authority over them call themselves Benefactors. But you are not to be like that. Instead, the greatest among you should be like the youngest, and the one who rules like the one who serves. For who is greater, the one who is at the table or the one who serves? Is it not the one who is at the table? But I am among you as one who serves. Luke 22:24-27

- Why do they let a stone sinner (unsaved) sing in the choir, just 'cause the Good Lord God done gave 'em a gift to sing … but they can't be bothered with getting' right first, 'fore they mess up our worship time with their unholy hollerin'. The Holy Ghost ain't so much impressed with your voice … as He be with your heart. **"Be not unequally yoked together with unbelievers; for what fellowship hath righteousness with unrighteousness? And what communion hath light with darkness?" 2nd Corinthians 6:14**

- Why do so many men of God seem so scared of a womenfolk who got the, sho'nuff, Holy Ghost … Jesus didn't much care who brought the word … or the healin' … or the blessin' to folks around 'em. I think Negro men been so beat down so bad … for so long … that they done learned to think that holdin' others down makes 'em somethin' more than they is ... and more than God wants 'em to be.

While he was at Bethany in the house of Simon the leper, as he sat at the table, a woman came with an alabaster jar of very costly ointment of nard, and she broke open the jar and poured the ointment on his head. But some were there who said to one another in anger, 'Why was the ointment wasted in this way? For this ointment could have been sold for more than three hundred denarii, and the money given to the poor.' And they scolded her. But Jesus said, 'Let her alone; why do you trouble her? She has performed a good service for me. For you always have the poor with you, and you can show kindness to them whenever you wish; but you will not always have me. She has done what she could; she has anointed my body beforehand for its burial. Truly I tell you, wherever the good news* is proclaimed in the whole world, what she has done will be told in remembrance of her.' John 12:1-9

- How come old folk ... well ... like me ... why they talk 'bout retirin' and kickin' back 'til they pass on? When God's ready to take me 'cross that Milky White Way, He gonna say, "Well done". But 'til then, we best understand that retirin' is for worldly folk. Us right Christians s'posta be doin' what the Good Lord God gifted us to do ... 'til the toil is done ... and the victory is won! We had our chance to rest back in the Garden ... but Adam and Eve done burst that bubble ... back when they let that serpent Satan get 'em in trouble. 'Stead of frettin' 'bout getting' retired ... they need to be frettin' 'bout getting' refired ... in the Holy Ghost!

Know ye not that they which run in a race run all, but one receiveth the prize? So run, that ye may obtain. 1st Corinthians 9:24

- Lord, I don't mind so much that somebody done took the time and trouble to type up a bunch of folded paper, to give folks when the walk into church on Sunday. But, for God's sake, do we gotta be scared to flip the script, if'n the Holy Ghost takes a notion to move the service this a way or that. After all, seems we talk 'bout invitin' Him in ... straight from the get ... every Sunday mornin' ... but then folks be scared to let Him breathe ... and if'n He don't breathe on us, all the power be gone. I s'pose some Pastors believe they the ones callin' the shots. Lord have mercy on 'em! **"And do not grieve the Holy Spirit of God, by whom you were sealed for the day of redemption." Ephesians 4:30**

- Why can't being a Christian set us free ... in our churches? Seems like the churches ain't nothin' but a dif-

ferent kinda prison … made by man … to serve man …
and keep the people of the Good Lord God from really
knowin' Him … once and for always … for theyselves.
LORD HELP 'EM!—**If the Son therefore shall make
you free, ye shall be free indeed. John 8:36**

*I believe I know the answer to ALL these questions. It's 'cause
we so messed up so much of the time. It's just a confirmation
'bout how bad we need Jesus … 'specially churchin' folk. I just
thank ya, Lord, that you give us discernment to see the difference and seize the light … whenever and wherever it shines …
and let the chips fall where they might. I know full well that
when I pass, my spirit gonna move on up … and my body …
the one you done lended me … gonna get laid on down … in a
box. But I mean to tell ya … I ain't lettin' no mere mortal …
man nor woman … box me up before my time … not so long
as the Holy Spirit got His breath on me … and in me … 'cause
I'm free … indeed.*

*Father, I know that's a lot of hard stuff to dump in your lap
today, but I also know that the Lord is able. I thank the Holy
Spirit for settin' me free … so's I can go to Church of the People
… see the mess … and still see you like I need to. We've had a
bunch of Pastors in the last fifty years … some better'n others
… but I pray to you now, Lord. Pierce their hearts … like Jesus
been pierced … and open their wounds to let His life-giving
blood wash on over 'em … when they get too high and too*

mighty. Touch their bodies, Father, so's they can understand 'bout other folks pain … and 'bout your healin' power. Open their minds, Holy Spirit, so's they can understand ALL your Word … and in new ways … throughout all their days. Tune their ears, Lord, so's they'll know the voice of the Holy Spirit tellin' 'em to be still … and wait for guidance … 'fore they pretend to know how to lead other folk. Sear their sin-sick souls, in the name of Jesus, so's they'll know for sure that You, Lord, are the onliest one that's all the way walkin' right … and the onliest one we'll ever need to lean on … in times of trouble.

Lord, I pray today that you receive confession from folk … folk who done made it their bidness to push other folk down, so's they can feel bigger. I see it in the church, Lord … and I been feelin' the daggers every day o' my life … whilst livin' in this crazy world run by white folks. I know Negro folk wear their wants on their sleeves and put each others bidness in the street … but white folks … po thangs … they likes to pretend their sins don't stink in your nostrils. Humble us all to surrender to you.

And last, oh God, help me whilst I'm here … to tend to and teach my sweet "Baby Grands" … that You don't make no junk … and You don't abide no bunk. Help my babies to call on you … first … before they jump on off and pull some fool mess. And to anybody, anywhere … whoever hears tell of my little stories 'bout me and the Church of the People … I hope

you understand right ... that you ... you my "Baby Grands"
too ... and Grandmama loves you ... real good!

EPILOUGUE

Children, you can come on in now. Grandmama done had a good talk with the Good Lord God, and it's past time to head on over to Church of the People for Tuesday Bible Study. One of you taller young'uns go up on yonder wall ... fetch me down my walkin' cane ... thank ya kindly. Now you older young'uns grab hold of them baby grand's little hands. Else they mightcould get hit up and runt over by a car or tractor ... or a hogwild hog ... and we done already had pancakes, ain't we? Now, I want all my children to make your Grandmama happy and sing along with me on my favorite song ... and sing it out proud ... so's you can drown out my caterwallin' ...

> *We're gonna walk ... walk that milky white way ...*
> *oh yes*
> *One of these days.*
> *Oh, I'm gonna walk ... that milky white way*
> *One of these days ... well, well, well, well.*
> *He's gonna take me ... up by my hand*
> *So's I can join in ... that Christian band.*
> *Yes, I'm gonna walk ... walk that milky white way*
> *... My lord*

One of these days ... one of these days.
I'm gonna see ... my dear old grandmother ... oh,
yes
When I get home.... .

In Jesus' Name ... AMEN, AMEN and AMEN!

ABOUT THE AUTHORS

Yvonne Cohen began writing this book shortly before she met and married Ben Cohen. But when he began reading the stories, his vivid vision of Grandmama's character led him to begin writing his own stories about the *Church of the People*. Most of the stories evolved collaboratively, in the hope and belief that this collection of parables could be enjoyed on different levels and by different kinds of people … perhaps as different as the unlikely pair of Christian writers of the book you hold now.

Yevonne Johnson was the 2nd child to an Arkansas-born African-American father, who never overcame the stress and shame of the Jim Crow south, even after he achieved middle-class status in Flint, Michigan. He was a violent, tyrannical drunk, who beat his wife and five children regularly. Her first book, *"A Miracle in the House"* chronicles her struggle to rise above the world's low expectations and her own deep circumstances. When Yvonne found Christ at age 27, she had a 10-year old son and more than a few poor choices to look back on. Needless to say, God cannot fail. Today Yvonne lives with her husband and a cat in Owings Mills, a suburb of Baltimore. She has a double Masters Degree, and trains human service workers to respond effectively to victims of family violence and dysfunction, including churches. She has authored several life skills manuals for vulnerable populations, such as, *"Fostering My Path to Independence"*, for foster children "aging out" of the system. Yevonne's joy is in her family, especially her three grandsons, and in her Lord. She periodically preaches, but only if she feels the congregation is ready to … "keep it *real*". She married Ben in 2004.

Benton Cohen was the middle child of three, born to Dr. Jonas Cohen in Northwest Baltimore City. Ben's Great, Great, Great Grandfather started the first Temple in Baltimore. In the midst of this middle-class Jewish "ghetto", a long-suffering, sickly little 5-year old received intervention, in the person of Mindella Scott Carr, the family's new live-in maid. Years later, Mindella explained to Ben that she would pray over him when his parents were out. Ben describes his parents as, a lukewarm Jewish father and a devoutly atheistic mother, who raised her children to be completely self-reliant. Both his mother and younger sister ended up committing suicide, and finally, at the age of 43, Ben came to, what he terms, "the end of himself" and found the faith to believe that he was inadequate to the task of self-reliance, in the face of the world he found around him. He accepted Jesus as his Lord and Savior. Today, after abandoning a 20-year career in marketing, Ben assists the poor and underemployed in finding jobs and he avidly collects and chronicles recordings of post-WWII African-American music ... an avocation reflected in many of the stories in this book.

Just remember, children ... don't never fool your own self into thinkin' God gonna always answer your ev'ry little prayer and bail out your boat for ya. He don't hold with no hypo-crites. Caint no grace, blood, faith or prayer save us from our sin, if'n that sin is still in our hearts ... 'cause doin' that grieves the Spirit ... and cleaves our access to His power.

Ye ask, and receive not, because ye ask amiss, that ye may consume it upon your lusts.

James 4:3

978-0-595-45450-1
0-595-45450-X

Made in the USA
Las Vegas, NV
02 April 2021